PENGUIN CLASSICS

# A VOCATION AND A VOICE

Kate O'Flaherty was born on February 8, 1850, in St. Louis, of French and Irish ancestry. She was graduated from the St. Louis Academy of the Sacred Heart in 1868; two years later she married Oscar Chopin and went to live with him in New Orleans. They had five sons by 1878, and the following year they moved to Cloutierville, a tiny French village in Natchitoches Parish, in northwest Louisiana. There their last child and only daughter was born in 1879. After Oscar's death in 1882, his widow ran their plantations and carried on a notorious romance with a married neighbor, but abruptly chose to return to St. Louis in 1884. Within five years she had begun her literary career, and during the next decade she published two novels—*At Fault* (1890) and *The Awakening* (1899)—and nearly a hundred short stories, poems, essays, plays, and reviews. Two volumes of short stories mostly set in the Cane River country of Louisiana, *Bayou Folk* (1894) and *A Night in Acadie* (1897), were acclaimed during her lifetime. But *The Awakening*, the story of a woman who has desires that marriage cannot fulfill, was widely condemned, and Chopin's publisher canceled her third short-story collection, *A Vocation and a Voice*. Chopin died on August 22, 1904.

Emily Toth is Professor of English and Director of Women's Studies at Louisiana State University, Baton Rouge. Her books include two biographies, *Kate Chopin* and *Inside Peyton Place: The Life of Grace Metalious*, and an award-winning novel, *Daughters of New Orleans*. She is also co-author of *The Curse: A Cultural History of Menstruation*; editor of *Regionalism and the Female Imagination*; and co-editor of *A Kate Chopin Miscellany* and its successor, *Kate Chopin's Private Papers*. She has published numerous articles on women's humor, popular culture, women writers, gossip, and related subjects.

# A VOCATION AND A VOICE

STORIES BY

Kate Chopin

*Edited and with an Introduction and Notes by Emily Toth*

PENGUIN BOOKS

PENGUIN BOOKS
Published by the Penguin Group
Penguin Books USA Inc.,
375 Hudson Street, New York, New York 10014, U.S.A.
Penguin Books Ltd, 27 Wrights Lane,
London W8 5TZ, England
Penguin Books Australia Ltd, Ringwood,
Victoria, Australia
Penguin Books Canada Ltd, 2801 John Street,
Markham, Ontario, Canada L3R 1B4
Penguin Books (N.Z.) Ltd, 182–190 Wairau Road,
Auckland 10, New Zealand

Penguin Books Ltd, Registered Offices:
Harmondsworth, Middlesex, England

This collection first published in Penguin Books 1991

9 10



LIBRARY OF CONGRESS CATALOGING IN PUBLICATION DATA
Chopin, Kate, 1851–1904.
A vocation and a voice/Kate Chopin; edited and with an
introduction and notes by Emily Toth.
p. cm.
Includes bibliographical references.
ISBN 0 14 03.9078 2
I. Toth, Emily, II. Title.
PS1294.C63A76 1991
813′.4—dc20 90–7798

Printed in the United States of America

# CONTENTS

# INTRODUCTION

"What do I write? Well, not everything that comes into my head," Kate Chopin declared in the *St. Louis Post-Dispatch* in November 1899. Seven months earlier, she had published *The Awakening*, a novel that scandalized readers with its heroine's adulterous desires—but it was hardly Kate Chopin's only unconventional work. Many of her most avant-garde and thought-provoking stories were to appear in *A Vocation and a Voice*, the short story collection that was slated for publication, and then canceled, in 1900. It is now being published, here, for the first time.

To her contemporaries, Kate Chopin was a beloved writer, acclaimed for her Louisiana local color stories in *Bayou Folk* (1894) and *A Night in Acadie* (1897). Her first novel, *At Fault* (1890), also has its happiest scenes in Louisiana. Throughout her literary career, Kate Chopin lived in St. Louis, but until she wrote the stories in *A Vocation and a Voice*, it was Louisiana that engaged her imagination and enticed her readers.

Born on February 8, 1850, Kate O'Flaherty was a St. Louisan by birth. Her mother, Eliza Faris, was of French descent and always spoke English with a French accent; her father, Thomas O'Flaherty, was an Irish immigrant and self-made man, twenty-three years older than his wife. Eliza, sixteen a few days before her wedding, brought social standing to the marriage, but she was penniless. Thomas's wealth provided for her family and cemented his own social position.

Five-year-old Katherine O'Flaherty, Eliza and Thomas's second child, entered boarding school at the Sacred Heart Academy in St. Louis in September 1855. But just two months later, on November 1, her father was one of the civic leaders on the gala inaugural train over the new Gasconade Bridge, linking St. Louis and Jefferson City. When the bridge suddenly collapsed, Thomas was killed—and Kate came home.

Nearly forty years later, Kate Chopin wrote about such a sudden death in "The Dream of an Hour" (now called "The Story of an Hour"), one of the tales in *A Vocation and a Voice*. In her story of a wife who hears that her husband has been killed in a railroad accident, Chopin recounted the cataclysmic event of her childhood (although in real life, there was no surprise ending). In her story, Chopin echoed the names from her childhood: her fictional wife is Louise, resembling the French pronunciation of Eliza, as it would have been overheard by a frightened little girl. Louise's sister is named Josephine, the name of Eliza O'Flaherty's youngest sister. Two men falsely reported killed at the Gasconade were named Bryan and Moore, and one of the dead was named Bullard: combining names and initials, Kate Chopin called the husband in her story Brently Mallard.

Chopin often used similar names as memory devices, spurs

to creativity, but "The Story of an Hour," like many of the *Vocation and a Voice* tales, is also a clever piece of social criticism, showing without preaching. Chopin's Louise has been a good wife, but she sees that death has freed her from sacrificing herself to someone else's will. Now she can make her own life.

As for Kate O'Flaherty, her father's death opened the door for the woman who shaped her early years (just as a woman inspires Alberta, the Nun in "Two Portraits"). At home Kate's great-grandmother, Victoria Verdon Charleville, taught her music (piano), French, and reading and writing, interspersed with gossip about local scandals and intrepid women. Madame Charleville's mother, for one, had obtained the first legal separation ever granted in Catholic St. Louis, and then went on to operate a very profitable shipping business. Madame Charleville, herself a widow, never remarried, nor did her daughter or her granddaughter, Eliza—so that Kate grew up in a household of lively, independent widows. There were also young aunts and uncles, two brothers and a sister, a boarder or two, and half a dozen slaves.

With her closest schoolgirl chum, Kitty Garesché, Kate shared candy and climbed trees (a mischievous pastime described in the story "Lilacs"). Passionate lovers of music and reading, Kate and Kitty read poetry together, enjoyed sentimental adventure stories, and devoured Sir Walter Scott's *Ivanhoe*, Grace Aguilar's *Days of Bruce*, and other romantic historical novels. St. Louis, with its fossil museums, circuses, and libraries, was a fascinating place for curious young girls and a mecca for scientific dabblers. The real-life Dr. George Engelmann, founder of a botanical society, and Dr. Friedrich Wizlizenus (known as "whistling Jesus") resemble the scientists Kate Chopin depicted much later in "A Mental Suggestion" and "An Easter Day Conversion (A Morning Walk)."

But in the 1850s, St. Louis was also a slave city in a slave state, and two months after Kate O'Flaherty's eleventh birthday, war broke out. Although Missouri did not secede from the Union, Kate endured martial law, sudden and frightening school closings, and the threat of arrest when she tore down a Yankee flag from the family porch. After the Union victory at Vicksburg, Yankee soldiers invaded her household and forced Eliza O'Flaherty, at bayonet point, to hoist their flag. The year 1863 was full of losses for young Kate: her teacher and great-grandmother Madame Charleville died; her half-brother George, a Confederate soldier, died; and her best friend, Kitty, was banished from St. Louis because her father supported the Confederacy. It was five years before the two friends saw each other again.

Then, in the peace after the war, Kate O'Flaherty became an honor student at the Sacred Heart Academy, where she was acclaimed for her essays and story telling. In her schoolgirl notebook, she collected apt quotations about women's rights, art, religion, music, and human foibles. She also sometimes expressed barbed opinions: on a sentimental greeting card, Kate scrawled, "Very pretty, but where's the point?"

After her graduation in 1868, Kate O'Flaherty entered St. Louis society, where she was popular for her musical talents, beauty, "amiability of character," and "cleverness." Yet in her diary, she complained about dancing till dawn with men "whose only talent lies in their feet." She disliked "general spreeing," because it kept her from her "dear reading and writing that I love so well." (Other people, she noted, thought she was very strange.)

By 1870 Kate O'Flaherty and Kitty Garesché, twenty-year-olds, had to choose directions for their lives. As in Chopin's "Two Portraits," they had come to the age at which "the languor of love creeps into the veins and dreams begin." Like Alberta the Nun, Kitty evidently felt "an overpowering impulse toward the purely spiritual": she joined the intellectually rigorous Sacred Heart nuns, embarking on a long career as a dedicated teacher. But Kate chose another path: "the right man," she called him in her diary.

Oscar Chopin, born in Louisiana in 1844, had lived in France during the war years. According to his own account, he spent much of his time ogling young women—and so failed his baccalaureate exam. But in postwar St. Louis, Oscar studied business in his great-uncle's firm and attended exquisite society parties at the Oakland estate, where he met Kate O'Flaherty. Theirs was a proper match: both were Catholic, spoke French, and had relatives in the Cane River country of Louisiana; they also shared an interest in music, literature, and word play.

After their wedding on June 9, 1870, in Holy Angels Church in St. Louis, the young Chopins set off on a three-month European honeymoon. Kate, reveling in their freedom, drank beer, walked about alone, and asked impertinent questions; she and Oscar skipped mass and resolved not to feel guilty. By the time the young Chopins settled in New Orleans in October, Kate was expecting her first child.

By 1878 the Chopins had five sons and a pretty home in the Garden District (now 1413–1415 Louisiana Avenue), but Oscar's business as a cotton factor was failing. To salvage what they could, the Chopins moved to his family lands in Cloutierville, (*Cloo-chy-ville*), a tiny village in Natchitoches (*Nack-i-tush*) Parish in northwest Louisiana. There Kate gave birth to Lélia, the last Chopin child and only daughter.

The Chopins lived in a large white house (now the Bayou Folk Museum/Kate Chopin home), and Kate amazed country people with her lavender riding habits and plumed hats from New Orleans. She lifted her skirts too high when she crossed the village's one street, displaying her ankles; she smoked Cuban cigarettes—something no lady did. ("An Egyptian Cigarette," one of the *Vocation and a Voice* stories, suggests that she smoked something stronger and stranger than tobacco—but that was years later.)

In 1882, another sudden loss transformed Kate Chopin's life: Oscar died of malaria, on December 10. His widow and six children were left some twelve thousand dollars in debt. Taking charge of her own life, as the widows in her family had always done, Kate sold some of the property, ran the plantations and general store herself, and attracted the attentions of a charming and wealthy neighboring planter. Albert Sampite (*SAM-pi-TAY*), who insinuated himself into her business affairs and her personal life, shared a love of horses and the night and an attraction to the forbidden. Their relationship became a notorious romance, which inspired the character named Alcée in two of her short stories and *The Awakening*.

But Albert Sampite had his failings. He drank too much, he was married, and he beat his wife (who later separated from him and always said that Kate Chopin had broken up her marriage). Abruptly, in 1884, Chopin and her children returned to St. Louis, to live with her mother.

Eliza O'Flaherty's death a year later plunged her daughter into a deep depression, until her friend and obstetrician, Frederick Kolbenheyer, suggested that Kate try writing professionally. Chopin's early stories set in St. Louis did not sell easily, but there was a ready market, she found, for stories of Louisiana life. And so Kate Chopin became the first writer to use the Cane River country of Louisiana, Natchitoches Parish, as her own fictional world. Within four years, Chopin was a published author, and by the mid-1890s, she was publishing in the most esteemed national magazines, including the *Century*, the *Atlantic*, and *Youth's Companion*.

Editors and readers applauded her stories of Louisiana country people, with their soft-sounding patois, fanciful French names, and quaint folkways. Chopin wrote about blacks and whites, Creoles and Acadians ("Cajuns"), and characters who were comical and passionate, honorable and sweet—and scarcely ever evil. Yet some of her earliest stories were chilling. In "Désirée's Baby," for instance, a plantation master casts off his devoted wife because he thinks she is black; in "La Belle Zoraïde," a slave woman deprived of her child goes mad with grief. But reviewers of Chopin's first collection, *Bayou Folk*, focused on local color and charm, ignoring her social criticism and the strong and independent female characters she was creating.

Chopin's second collection, *A Night in Acadie*, received much less attention. Although its stories were also set in Louisiana, they were vignettes, slices of life in which wives looked curiously at other men and sudden deaths meant cheerful new possibilities. Reviewers were puzzled by the stories, which did not end neatly: some trailed off, without really concluding at all. Kate Chopin was no longer telling stories in a traditional way, and some reviewers wished that she would return to the sunny charm of *Bayou Folk*.

But *Vogue*, a new magazine in the 1890s, was publishing Chopin's most advanced stories, the ones exploding romantic myths. Under its strong-minded, eccentric, and progressive editor, Josephine Redding, *Vogue* was never limited to stories suitable for "the Young Person," the mythical sheltered adolescent who, most editors said, had to be protected from unseemly magazine matter.

Kate Chopin, her St. Louis friend Charles Deyo once noted, did not write for "the young person" but for "seasoned souls," and her *Vogue* stories were about adult realities. Of the twenty-two stories planned for *A Vocation and a Voice*, ten first appeared in *Vogue:* "An Egyptian Cigarette," "The White Eagle," "The Story of an Hour," "Two Summers and Two Souls," "The Unexpected," "Her Letters," "The Kiss," "Suzette," "The Recovery," and "The Blind Man." Many involve blindness or death; others hint broadly at "guilty love" (sex outside marriage), a subject untouchable in most American magazines.

With *A Vocation and a Voice*, stories she began writing as early as 1893, Kate Chopin abandoned Louisiana as a setting and local color as a mode of expression. Only four tales take place in Louisiana; only two ("Suzette" and "Ti Démon") rely on dialects and local lore. In "The Godmother," Chopin makes the Natchitoches Parish setting incidental to a deadly tale of murder and misguided loyalty, while in "A Vocation and a Voice," she implies a Louisiana setting for part of the story, by mentioning bayous, crawfish, and " 'Cadians" (Cajuns)—but the story is about a boy's consciousness, not about Louisiana ways. Most of the other stories in *A Vocation and a Voice* have no definable setting, except for two in rural Missouri ("Elizabeth Stock's One Story" and "Juanita") and one in Paris ("Lilacs").

Chopin had written all but two of the *Vocation and a Voice* stories (the second "Ti Démon" and "The White Eagle") before *The Awakening* appeared in April 1899, published by the innovative Herbert S. Stone & Company in Chicago. For several years, publishers and editors had urged Chopin to write a novel, claiming it would bring her more money and recognition than her short stories.

But *The Awakening* elicited hostile, even damning reviews. Although it was never banned or withdrawn from libraries (that myth grew up later), Kate Chopin's story of a discontented wife and mother who yearns for freedom, artistic fulfillment, and other men offended reviewers throughout the United States. In

St. Louis, it was called "too strong drink for moral babes—should be labeled 'poison' "; it was said to make readers "sick of human nature." In other cities, reviewers found *The Awakening* "repellent," promoting "unholy imaginations" and "unclean desires," with a plot "that can hardly be described in language fit for publication."

St. Louis women did rally to Kate Chopin, writing her fond letters of praise and honoring her at the city's most prestigious women's club, the Wednesday Club, where she read "Ti Démon," seven months after *The Awakening* appeared. The story was well received, and three Chopin poems were also set to music for the occasion.

But in February 1900, Herbert S. Stone & Company canceled Kate Chopin's contract; they would not publish her third short story collection, *A Vocation and a Voice*. Herbert Stone did not actually say that *The Awakening*'s notoriety had caused him to cancel *A Vocation and a Voice*; apparently he gave Kate Chopin no reason at all and let her assume the worst. (In fact, Stone was cutting back on the firm's list and not necessarily making a judgment on Chopin's work.) Lucy Monroe, the editor who had championed *The Awakening*, seems not to have influenced Stone to keep *A Vocation and a Voice*.

Stone had known that Kate Chopin was no traditional American writer. Although she admired stories by the New Englanders Sarah Orne Jewett and Mary E. Wilkins, Chopin was most inspired by the work of a Frenchman, Guy de Maupassant, whose subtlety and indirection she studied and imitated. Between 1894 and 1898, she also translated eight of his stories but managed to sell only the most conventional three. The others, which include a woman's intimate love for her horse and a man's "strange sexual perversion" with flowers, were far too graphic for American magazines. The brooding Maupassant tales, which Chopin called "Mad Stories," were about suicide, death, water, night dreams, infidelity—the subjects Chopin herself used in *A Vocation and a Voice*.

Kate Chopin's writing was also influenced by the friends who frequented her salon, held at her unpretentious home at 3317 Morgan Street (now Delmar, but the house no longer exists). Although one visitor called her "the most brilliant, distinguished, and interesting woman that has ever graced St. Louis," Chopin did not dominate at her "Thursdays": "One realizes only afterward how many good and witty things she has said in the course of the conversation," another friend recalled.

Her guests were outspoken and argumentative authors, artists, and editors. Dr. Kolbenheyer, an agnostic and an anarchist, would declaim about the filth and "bestiality" of Polish peasant life; William Vincent Byars, a poet and linguist, could groan "Ah me!" in half a dozen languages. Carrie Blackman, a beautiful, dark-eyed, pensive artist whose husband adored her, appeared to have a troubling and mysterious secret (or so Kate Chopin noted in her own diary). Blackman, best known for her portrait of a woman reading letters, seems to have inspired Chopin's story "Her Letters."

Chopin's women friends were not ordinary, nor were they society "philistines": she inveighed against those in her diary. In "The Kiss," she skewers the socialite Nathalie, who kisses for pleasure but marries for money. For her own friends, Chopin preferred such women as the flamboyant Rosa Sonneschein, who wore theatrical costumes, founded the Pioneers (the first literary society for Jewish women), and created a scandal by divorcing her rabbi husband—after which she started *The American Jewess*, the first magazine by and for Jewish women.

The only gentile contributor to her first issue was her fellow cigar-smoker, Kate Chopin.

Chopin also sneaked secret cigarettes with the globetrotting journalist Florence Hayward, a clever humor writer and a proud, self-proclaimed "independent spinster." Hayward resembled, physically, the haughty central character in "The Falling in Love of Fedora"—but her no-nonsense ideas and mental poise are more like those of Pauline in "A Mental Suggestion." Another Chopin friend, Sue V. Moore, edited *St. Louis Life* and used it to boost Kate Chopin—by announcing her literary breakthroughs, publishing her reviews and translations, and writing an admiring profile that was frequently reprinted.

At her salon, at musicales (where she played the piano), and at al fresco suppers, Kate Chopin enjoyed the company of "a pink-red group of intellectuals," her son Felix used to say. (He also claimed that they "expressed their independence by wearing eccentric clothing," but no photographs survive.) Her friends' telling ghost stories and debating new scientific theories no doubt influenced Kate Chopin to write her gently satirical story of hypnosis, "A Mental Suggestion." She also drew on life for her beliefs about extrasensory perception: one evening, sensing that something had happened to her daughter, Chopin raced home and found that there had indeed been a dangerous fire.

Other fires simmered. Among Chopin and her male admirers, most of whom were married, there were sometimes sexual tensions. Two editors at the *St. Louis Post-Dispatch,* John Dillon and George Johns, were close Chopin friends and perhaps more. Also, according to Chopin's son Felix, "Kolby had eyes for Mom," although the fierce-eyed, dark-bearded doctor remained married to his childhood sweetheart. Whether Kate

Chopin had eyes for Frederick Kolbenheyer is unknown, but her doctor characters are often the ones with the greatest interest in human peculiarities and wicked ways.

Chopin welcomed at least one notorious character to her circle: William Marion Reedy, the rotund and raffish editor of the weekly *St. Louis Mirror*. Reedy published groundbreaking authors few others would touch, among them Oscar Wilde and Theodore Dreiser. Kate Chopin once gave Billy Reedy a box of his favorite cigars for Christmas, and she was one of few St. Louisans who did not condemn him. A former altar boy from Kerry Patch (the Irish ghetto), and known for his sweet voice and angelic face, Reedy had succumbed to alcoholic and sexual temptations: during one binge he married a famous St. Louis madam. After divorce and remarriage, he was excommunicated, and he shared Kate Chopin's fierce insistence on the right to divorce.

Reedy published Chopin's stories, said she belonged in an American academy of letters, and called her one of St. Louis's "Minervas," women most esteemed for intellectual achievements. Reedy also inspired Chopin's longest short story, "A Vocation and a Voice," in which a poor, nameless altar boy from Kerry Patch runs off with vagabonds, and a whole new world of music and sensuality opens to him. Perhaps to amuse or humor the adult Reedy, who loved sonorous Latinate words, Chopin uses a much more pompous vocabulary than was her wont: her boy wears, for instance, "habiliments" and "canonicals" instead of "clothes" and "robes." Evidently, the boy's seduction by the gypsyish Suzima, a few days after he has come upon her naked in a stream, was too racy for almost all magazine editors—but not for Reedy, who published it in his *Mirror*.

Like Reedy, Kate Chopin read the newest, most modern European writers, among them Ibsen, Tolstoy, and Swinburne.

When her eyes ailed her, a friend read to her from the Norwegian Alexander Kielland's *Tales of Two Countries*—and Kielland's description of a trapped bird with wise, all-knowing eyes anticipates "The White Eagle." (The story also resembles Flaubert's "A Simple Heart.") But unlike her European models, Kate Chopin loved the scents, the sights, the sounds of nature, and her stories are full of caressing breezes, delicious aromas, and the colors of light and life. *A Vocation and a Voice* is a celebration of the senses over the intellect, and eros over reason.

Chopin also evidently experimented with altered states of consciousness and was intrigued by Eastern religions and Oriental luxury. In "An Egyptian Cigarette," the story of a drug trip, the narrator has visions of lilies and garlands, pagan gods, waters, birds, and death—images also found in *The Awakening* but highly uncommon in the Midwest or in American literature in the late nineteenth century.

Kate Chopin was an imaginer and a questioner who had stopped going to church not long after her mother's death, and her salon was peopled by nonconformists who ignored or derided organized religion. But there were parts of the religious life that she still found appealing. In "Lilacs," Chopin describes the Sacred Heart rituals she knew as a child: the protagonist, now a very worldly Parisian actress, still remembers how to fold her clothes with dainty correctness, and at certain times of the year, she yearns for the nuns' serene, untroubled life. But four days after writing "Lilacs," Kate Chopin visited a school friend, Liza, who had become a Sacred Heart nun. The peace of convent life was attractive, Chopin wrote in her diary, and Liza had "her lover in the dark" (Jesus)—but to Chopin that convent world was "a phantasmagoria," not real life.

A year later, when she wrote "Two Portraits," Chopin had

come to a far more radical thought: that nuns had not truly surrendered their earthly desires and human passions. Alberta the Nun, after all, is known for her "visions" and her "ecstasies." Then, a year after that, Chopin wrote "A Vocation and a Voice," in which the pure spiritual singing of the boy earns him and his vagabond companions, a fortune teller and a fraudulent herbal healer, the most tangible reward of all: money.

Like most nineteenth-century women writers, Kate Chopin claimed to have no serious ideas or ambitions, but in fact she was a dedicated professional who studied the markets and sought good pay as well as literary distinction (although she never earned a living from her writings). She seems to have enjoyed motherhood: her children, in their twenties by the time *A Vocation and a Voice* was to appear, adored her and never wanted to leave home, and she worried about them. During the months after her son Fred joined the troops fighting the Spanish-American War, Chopin could write only sad tales, including "Ti Démon (A Horse Story)" and "Elizabeth Stock's One Story." No magazine would publish either one: evidently they lacked the optimism American editors favored.

After *A Vocation and a Voice* was canceled, Kate Chopin wrote very little. The title story, printed in Reedy's *Mirror* in 1902, proved to be the last adult story that Chopin would publish. Her health was deteriorating; her friends and relatives were ailing and dying; and her son Jean's wife died in childbirth, plunging him into a depression from which he never recovered. Chopin moved to a smaller home (still extant, at 4232 McPherson), and she apparently gave up her salon.

After a strenuous day at the St. Louis World's Fair, she died of a brain hemorrhage on August 22, 1904, and was buried in Calvary Cemetery with a lilac bush, her favorite flower, shadowing her gravestone. One obituary reported that a collection of Chopin short stories was to be published the following year, but *A Vocation and a Voice* never appeared.

*The Awakening* soon went out of print; "Désirée's Baby," repeatedly anthologized, was virtually all that was remembered of Kate Chopin. Daniel S. Rankin, in his often-inaccurate *Kate Chopin and Her Creole Stories* (1932), listed the tales that were to appear in *A Vocation and a Voice*—but whether he listed their order correctly cannot be known. Nor can we know whether "Ti Démon" in Rankin's list refers to Chopin's March 1898 story with that title (later called "A Horse Story," after its central character)—or to her November 1899 "Ti Démon," in which the title character is a man. Of the eleven Chopin stories that Rankin published, seven were from *A Vocation and a Voice*, and one ("Two Portraits") had never been in print before.

When, in the 1960s, the Norwegian scholar Per Seyersted discovered Chopin's writings, he edited her *Complete Works* and restored her to American literature—at a time when American women were ready to appreciate, and embrace, an earlier supporter of women's possibilities.

Yet even today Kate Chopin is not known for the stories in *A Vocation and a Voice.* Only "The Story of an Hour" (filmed twice and constantly reprinted) is read often, although "Elizabeth Stock's One Story" and "The Godmother" are also devastating critiques of the ideal of womanly self-sacrifice. Chopin's most-anthologized stories are still the *Bayou Folk* stories, set in Louisiana, about marriage and motherhood and unfulfilled sexual longings—but her *Vocation and a Voice* stories are, in many ways, her most modern achievements.

Chopin experimented with form as well as content. "An Idle Fellow" and "The Night Came Slowly" are meditations rather than stories, and the title character in "Elizabeth Stock's One

Story" concedes that her own literary efforts seem to lack plots. But "The Falling in Love of Fedora," rejected by the *Atlantic* in the 1890s for having "scarcely any story at all," now lends itself to many psychoanalytic interpretations, and the Wanton in "Two Portraits" is a stunningly accurate portrayal of a battered child. The other *Vocation and a Voice* stories, rarely reprinted and scarcely known, reveal other facets of Kate Chopin: as social critic and as deep thinker about obsession and melancholy, ripeness and decay.

Kate Chopin wrote the *Vocation and a Voice* stories between 1893 ("An Idle Fellow") and 1900 ("The White Eagle"), but most were clustered between 1894–1896, the years of her greatest productivity as an author. In her study, lined with bookshelves and adorned with a statue of a naked Venus, Chopin wrote quickly and rarely revised. Often she completed a story in one sitting, and her notebook lists just one day for the composition of most of the *Vocation and a Voice* stories. But "Lilacs" took three days; "The Godmother" took two months; and for a few others, including "A Vocation and a Voice" and "An Egyptian Cigarette," Chopin listed only the month in which she finished the story.

A typical *Vocation and a Voice* story is surprising, a revelation of secrets and passions that do not quite mesh. Possibly only "A Mental Suggestion" and "An Easter Day Conversion (A Morning Walk)" might be considered happily-ever-after stories, but many other tales have touches of wry humor—and raise tantalizing questions. Sometimes the characters are disillusioned; sometimes they see all too clearly the blindnesses of others and connive around them. Nathalie, in "The Kiss," for instance, thinks she can flirt with one man even after marrying another—but has to console herself with her new husband "and his million."

In *A Vocation and a Voice*, romances usually go awry. Illnesses and aging change people and make them shrink from one another; for some, months apart make hearts grow fonder, but for others, out of sight means out of mind. Romances falter because the timing is wrong in at least seven stories: "Suzette," "The Kiss," "A Mental Suggestion," "Two Summers and Two Souls," "The Unexpected," "The Recovery," and "Ti Démon." Faithful husbands, as in "Her Letters," are rewarded with endless grief; independent-minded young women, as in "Suzette" and "The Unexpected," are appalled and wearied by importunate suitors.

Sensuality in *A Vocation and a Voice* is rarely romantic, sometimes mercantile, and occasionally quirky. Alberta, the Wanton in "Two Portraits," takes a lover simply because she thinks she is old enough, and she learns to sell her body for gold. The supercilious Fedora, infatuated with a young man in "The Falling in Love of Fedora," impulsively kisses his sister instead. (Possibly there was a real-life parallel, close to home: Chopin published that story in a St. Louis magazine under a pseudonym, "La Tour.") Likewise, the title character in "Juanita," based on a real-life rural Missouri postmaster's daughter, is no traditional heroine. A popular and sought-after beauty, weighing over two hundred pounds of "substantial flesh," Juanita attracts countless suitors—but runs off with a poor, shabby, one-legged man to whom she may or may not be married.

The *Vocation and a Voice* stories also examine organized religion. Both "Lilacs" and the Nun (in "Two Portraits") show that the cloistered life has a charming, graceful routine from which passion has not been entirely banished. But in "The Night Came Slowly," Chopin calls a man with his "Bible Class" "detestable" and "a young fool," and asks, "What does he know of Christ?" In "A Vocation and a Voice," the boy finally heeds his senses, not his creeds. Yet Chopin was not above writing an inspirational religious story that would sell: in "An Easter Conversion (A Morning Walk)," the sight of a girl with flowers awakens an oblivious man to the delights and sweetness of the world around him, and he finds himself in church.

But like the "Mad Stories" of Guy de Maupassant, Kate Chopin's stories in *A Vocation and a Voice* are more apt to be about obsessions. In "Two Summers and Two Souls," "Suzette," and "The Unexpected," a suitor's raving speech and intense eyes terrify his sweetheart. In "Her Letters," the husband can think of only one secret that his late wife might have wanted to take to the grave with her—and that secret destroys him. In "The Recovery," a woman obsessed with regaining her sight finally does not like what she sees, for she has been robbed of her illusions. Virtually every story in *A Vocation and a Voice* mentions eyes, at a time when Kate Chopin was having trouble with her own eyesight. (Her last portrait, a newspaper sketch by her son Oscar in late 1900, is the only picture of her wearing eyeglasses.)

Some stories in *A Vocation and a Voice* are also criticisms of capitalism, urban anomie, and blight in an age of robber barons. Because Chopin herself lived on a modest income from real-estate holdings, the 1900 United States census lists her occupation as "capitalist"—but she did not profit from the financial panics, the strikes, and the growing abyss separating poor and rich in the 1890s.

In *A Vocation and a Voice*, "The Kiss" and "Elizabeth Stock's One Story" both unmask the "plutocrats" whose cruelty Chopin's friends deplored. "A Vocation and a Voice" contrasts the charm and freedom of country life with the cold, hunger, and squalor of Kerry Patch. And in "The Blind Man," Chopin overturns readers' expectations by not making the poor blind man the victim of a trolley's progress through town—yet scarcely anyone who sees him knows or cares what happens to him. The only act of kindness comes when a policeman "considerately refrained from clubbing him."

Today Kate Chopin is best known for her portrayals of women, and *A Vocation and a Voice* includes many memorable female characters. The adventurous narrator who smokes the hallucinogenic cigarette in "An Egyptian Cigarette" is a woman, called "Madam" by her drug-producing friend; Suzima, the self-made "Egyptian Maid, the Wonder of the Orient," is the most colorful character in "A Vocation and a Voice." The nuns in "Lilacs" are winsome souls, naive and loving toward their worldly visitor. The most pathetic characters are the victimized women, such as Elizabeth Stock, Tante Elodie in "The Godmother," and the nameless girl in "The White Eagle." The most aggressive characters are also women, such as the actress Adrienne in "Lilacs" and Nathalie in "The Kiss." Like Louise in "The Story of an Hour," Chopin's women characters are able to dream past the present reality—although they rarely achieve their dreams.

The stories in *A Vocation and a Voice* round out our knowledge of Kate Chopin and her world. A handsome woman who loved creature comforts (cards, coffee, cigarettes), she wrote in her last story collection about sufferers—from cold, physical ailments, mental infirmities. The order of the stories suggests that she was unhappy: the joyous, pagan release of "A Vocation and a Voice," with its celebration of nature, music, and passion, leads into the despairing "Elizabeth Stock's One Story"; stories of pleasure shade quickly into tales of strangeness and woe; and the last story, "The Godmother," ends in lonely darkness.

But Kate Chopin also wrote about those who appreciate some of the things she most enjoyed: "a magnetic sympathetic hand clasp," a quiet walk at night: "And then, there are so many ways of saying good night!"

In this, her last short story collection, Kate Chopin is at last able to say good night to her readers. She finishes her vocation in her own voice.

# SUGGESTIONS FOR FURTHER READING

## The Works of Kate Chopin

Seyersted, Per, ed. *The Complete Works of Kate Chopin*. Baton Rouge: Louisiana State University Press, 1969.

Seyersted, Per, and Emily Toth, eds. *A Kate Chopin Miscellany*. Oslo and Natchitoches: Universitetsforlaget and Northwestern State University Press of Louisiana, 1979.

Toth, Emily, and Per Seyersted, eds. *Kate Chopin's Private Papers*. Bloomington: Indiana University Press, 1992. Updates and supersedes *A Kate Chopin Miscellany*.

## Biographies

Rankin, Daniel. *Kate Chopin and Her Creole Stories.* Philadelphia: University of Pennsylvania Press, 1932.

Seyersted, Per. *Kate Chopin: A Critical Biography.* Baton Rouge: Louisiana State University Press, and Oslo: Universitetsforlaget, 1969.

Toth, Emily. *Kate Chopin.* New York: William Morrow, 1990.

## Biographical Articles

Chopin, Felix. "Statement on Kate Chopin," January 19, 1949. Interview with Felix Chopin (Kate's son), notes taken by Charles van Ravenswaay of the Missouri Historical Society. In *Kate Chopin's Private Papers* and *A Kate Chopin Miscellany.*

Johns, Orrick. "The 'Cadians." *Mirror* XX (July 20, 1911), 5–6. In *Kate Chopin's Private Papers* and *A Kate Chopin Miscellany.*

(Knapp, Vernon). "Is There an Interesting Woman in St. Louis?" *St. Louis Republic*, September 11, 1910, part 5, 1. In *Kate Chopin's Private Papers* and *A Kate Chopin Miscellany.*

Mills, Elizabeth Shown. "Colorful Characters from Kate's Past." *Kate Chopin Newsletter* 2:1 (Spring 1976), 7–12.

Moore, Sue V. "Mrs. Kate Chopin." *St. Louis Life* 10 (June 9, 1894), 11–12. In *Kate Chopin's Private Papers* and *A Kate Chopin Miscellany.*

Schuyler, William. "Kate Chopin." *The Writer* VII (August 1894), 115–117. In *Kate Chopin's Private Papers* and *A Kate Chopin Miscellany.*

Toth, Emily. "A New Biographical Approach." In *Approaches to Teaching Kate Chopin's "The Awakening"*, ed. Bernard J. Koloski. New York: Modern Language Association of America, 1988, 60–66.

Wilson, Maryhelen. "Kate Chopin's Family: Fallacies and Facts, Including Kate's True Birthdate." *Kate Chopin Newsletter* 2 (Winter 1976–77), 25–31.

## Criticism

Arner, Robert D. "Kate Chopin." *Louisiana Studies* (Spring 1975). Entire issue devoted to Kate Chopin.

Bonner, Thomas Jr. "Christianity and Catholicism in the Fiction of Kate Chopin." *Southern Quarterly* 20 (Winter 1982), 118–125.

———. *The Kate Chopin Companion, with Chopin's Translations from French Fiction.* Westport: Greenwood Press, 1988.

———. "Kate Chopin's European Consciousness." *American Literary Realism* 8 (Summer 1975), 281–284.

Culley, Margaret, ed. *The Awakening: An Authoritative Text, Contexts, Criticism.* New York: Norton, 1976.

Donovan, Josephine. "Feminist Style Criticism." In *Images of Women in Fiction: Feminist Perspectives*, ed. Susan Koppelman Cornillon. Bowling Green: Popular Press, 1972, 344–348.

Dyer, Joyce Coyne. "Night Images in the Work of Kate Chopin." *American Literary Realism* 14 (1981), 216–230.

Ewell, Barbara C. *Kate Chopin.* New York: Ungar, 1986.

Holditch, W. Kenneth, ed. *In Old New Orleans.* Jackson: University Press of Mississippi, 1983.

Howell, Elmo. "Kate Chopin and the Pull of Faith: A Note on

'Lilacs.' " *Southern Studies* 18 (Spring 1979), 103–109.

Idol, John L. "A Note on William Marion Reedy and Kate Chopin." *Missouri Historical Society Bulletin* 30 (October 1973), 57–58.

Johns, Orrick. *The Time of Our Lives: The Story of My Father and Myself.* New York: Stackpole, 1937.

Jones, Anne Goodwyn. *Tomorrow Is Another Day: The Woman Writer in the South, 1859–1936.* Baton Rouge: Louisiana State University, 1981.

Koloski, Bernard J., ed. *Approaches to Teaching Kate Chopin's "The Awakening."* New York: Modern Language Association of America, 1988.

Miner, Madonne M. "Veiled Hints: An Affective Stylist's Reading of Kate Chopin's 'Story of an Hour.' " *Markham Review* II (Winter 1983), 29–32.

Primm, James Neal. *Lion of the Valley: St. Louis, Missouri.* Boulder, Colorado: Pruett Publishing Company, 1981.

Putzel, Max. *The Man in the Mirror: William Marion Reedy and His Magazine.* Cambridge: Harvard, 1963.

Seyersted, Per. "Kate Chopin: An Important St. Louis Writer Reconsidered." *Missouri Historical Society Bulletin* 19 (January 1963), 89–114.

———. "Kate Chopin's Wound: Two New Letters." *American Literary Realism* 20:1 (Fall 1987), 71–75.

Skaggs, Peggy. "The Boy's Quest in 'A Vocation and a Voice.' " *American Literature* 51 (1979), 270–276.

———. *Kate Chopin.* Boston: G. K. Hall, 1985.

———. " 'The Man-Instinct of Possession': A Persistent Theme in Kate Chopin's Stories." *Louisiana Studies* 14 (1975), 277–285.

Springer, Marlene. *Edith Wharton and Kate Chopin: A Reference Guide.* Boston: G. K. Hall, 1976.

———. "Kate Chopin: A Reference Guide Updated." *Resources for American Literary Study* II (1981), 25–42.

Toth, Emily. "The Independent Woman and 'Free' Love." *Massachusetts Review* 16 (Autumn 1975), 647–664.

———. "Kate Chopin and Literary Convention: 'Désirée's Baby.' " *Southern Studies* 20:2 (Summer 1981), 201–208.

———. "Kate Chopin's New Orleans Years." *New Orleans Review* 15:1 (Spring 1988), 53–60.

———. "Kate Chopin's *The Awakening* as Feminist Criticism." *Louisiana Studies* 15 (Fall 1976), 241–251.

———. "St. Louis and the Fiction of Kate Chopin." *Missouri Historical Society Bulletin* 32 (October 1975), 33–50.

———. "The Shadow of the First Biographer: The Case of Kate Chopin." *Southern Review* 26:2 (Spring 1990), 285–292.

———. "Timely and Timeless: The Treatment of Time in *The Awakening* and *Sister Carrie*." *Southern Studies* 16 (Fall 1977), 271–276.

Ziff, Larzer. *The American 1890s: Life and Times of a Lost Generation*. New York: Viking, 1966.

# A NOTE ON THE TEXT

The texts of all but one of the stories reprinted here are taken from Per Seyersted's definitive *The Complete Works of Kate Chopin*, published in two volumes by Louisiana State University Press in 1969. "Ti Démon (A Horse Story)" was first published in *A Kate Chopin Miscellany* (Northwestern State University of Louisiana and the University of Oslo, 1979) and reprinted in *Kate Chopin's Private Papers* (Indiana University Press, 1992), both edited by Emily Toth and Per Seyersted.

The list of stories to be published under the title *A Vocation and a Voice* appears in Daniel Rankin's *Kate Chopin and Her Creole Stories* (1932), the first Chopin biography. This edition follows the order of Rankin's list. Chopin wrote two stories using the title "Ti Démon," and both are reprinted here. The earlier one (written March 1898) was later retitled "A Horse Story"; the second, from November 1899, is probably the one

Chopin intended for her collection, but we cannot be sure.

For three other stories, there are alternative titles: the story Chopin published as "The Dream of an Hour" is now better known as "The Story of an Hour," its title in *The Complete Works of Kate Chopin.* The story that Chopin called "Fedora" (its title in *The Complete Works*) was published as "The Falling in Love of Fedora. A Sketch," under the pen name "La Tour." The story that Chopin called "A Morning Walk" (its title in *The Complete Works*) was published as "An Easter Day Conversion."

After each story, the date of composition and date and place of first publication are listed.

# A VOCATION AND A VOICE

# A VOCATION AND A VOICE

## I

"Is this Adams avenue?" asked a boy whose apparel and general appearance marked him as belonging to the lower ranks of society. He had just descended from a street car which had left the city an hour before, and was now depositing its remnant of passengers at the entrance of a beautiful and imposing suburban park.

"Adams avenue?" returned the conductor. "No this is Woodland Park. Can't you see it ain't any avenue? Adams is two miles northeast o'here. Th' Adams avenue car turned north on Dennison, just ahead of us, a half hour ago. You must a' taken the wrong car."

The boy was for a moment perplexed and undecided. He stood a while staring towards the northeast, then, thrusting his hands into his pockets, he turned and walked into the park.

He was rather tall, though he had spoken with the high, treble voice of a girl. His trousers were too short and so were the sleeves of his ill-fitting coat. His brown hair, under a shabby, felt cap, was longer than the prevailing fashion demanded, and his eyes were dark and quiet; they were not alert and seeking mischief, as the eyes of boys usually are.

The pockets into which he had thrust his hands were empty—quite empty; there was not so much as a penny in either of them. This was a fact which gave him cause for some reflection, but apparently no uneasiness. Mrs. Donnelly had given him but the five cents; and her mother, to whom he had been sent to deliver a message of some domestic purport, was expected to pay his return fare. He realized that his own lack of attention had betrayed him into the strait in which he found himself, and that his own ingenuity would have to extricate him. The only device which presented itself to him as possible, was to walk back to "The Patch," or out to Mrs. Donnelly's mother's.

It would be night before he could reach either place; he did not know the way anywhere; he was not accustomed to long and sustained walks. These considerations, which he accepted as final, gave him a comfortable sense of irresponsibility.

It was the late afternoon of an October day. The sun was warm and felt good to his shoulders through the old coat which he wore. There was a soft breeze blowing, seemingly from every quarter, playing fantastic tricks with the falling and fallen leaves that ran before him helter-skelter as he walked along the beaten, gravel path. He thought they looked like little live things, birds with disabled wings making the best of it in a mad frolic. He could not catch up with them; they ran on before him. There was a fine sweep of common to one side which gave an impression of space and distance, and men and boys were playing ball there. He did not turn in that direction or even more than glance at the ball-players, but wandered aimlessly across the grass towards the water and sat down upon a bench.

With him was a conviction that it would make no difference to any one whether he got back to "The Patch" or not. The Donnelly household, of which he formed an alien member, was overcrowded for comfort. The few dimes which he earned did not materially swell its sources of income. The seat which he occupied in the parish school for an hour or two each day would not remain long vacant in his absence. There were a dozen boys or more of his neighborhood who would serve Mass as ably as he, and who could run Father Doran's errands and do the priest's chores as capably. These reflections embodied themselves in a vague sense of being unessential which always dwelt with him, and which permitted him, at that moment, to abandon himself completely to the novelty and charm of his surroundings.

He stayed there a very long time, seated on the bench, quite still, blinking his eyes at the rippling water which sparkled in the rays of the setting sun. Contentment was penetrating him at every pore. His eyes gathered all the light of the waning day and the russet splendor of the Autumn foliage. The soft wind caressed him with a thousand wanton touches, and the scent of the earth and the trees—damp, aromatic,—came pleasantly to him mingled with the faint odor of distant burning leaves. The blue-gray smoke from a smoldering pile of leaves rolled in lazy billows among the birches on a far slope.

How good it was to be out in the open air. He would have liked to stay there always, far from the noise and grime of "The Patch." He wondered if Heaven might not be something like this, and if Father Doran was not misled in his conception of a celestial city paved with gold.

He sat blinking in the sun, almost purring with contentment. There were young people out in boats and others making merry on the grass near by. He looked at them, but felt no desire to join in their sports. The young girls did not attract him more than the boys or the little children. He had lapsed into a blessed state of tranquility and contemplation which seemed native to him. The sordid and puerile impulses of an existence which was not living had retired into a semi-oblivion in which he seemed to have no share. He belonged under God's sky in the free and open air.

When the sun had set and the frogs were beginning to croak in the waste places, the boy got up and stretched and relaxed his muscles which had grown cramped from sitting so long and so still. He felt that he would like to wander, even then, further into the Park, which looked to his unaccustomed eye like a dense forest across the water of the artificial lake. He would like to penetrate beyond into the open country where there were fields and hills and long stretches of wood. As he turned to leave the place he determined within himself that he would speak to Father Doran and ask the priest to assist him in obtaining employment somewhere in the country, somewhere that he might breathe as freely and contentedly as he had been doing for the past hour here in Woodland Park.

## II

In order to regain "The Patch" there was nothing for the boy to do but follow the track of the car which had brought him so far from his destination. He started out resolutely, walking between the tracks, taking great strides with his long, growing legs and looking wistfully after each car as he stepped out of the way of its approach. Here and there he passed an imposing mansion in the dusk, splendid and isolated. There were long stretches of vacant land which enterprising dealers had laid out in building lots. Sometimes he left the track and walked along the line of a straggling fence behind which were market-gardens, the vegetables all in stiff geometrical designs and colorless in the uncertain light.

There were few people abroad; an occasional carriage rolled by, and workingmen, more fortunate than he, occupied the cars that went jangling along. He sat for awhile at the back of a slow-moving wagon, dropping down into the dust when it turned out of his course.

The boy, as he labored along in the semi-darkness that was settling about him, at once became conscious that he was very hungry. It was the odor of frying bacon and the scent of coffee somewhere near that had suddenly made him aware of the fact.

At no great distance from the road he saw a canvas-covered wagon and a small tent, the rude paraphernalia of "movers." A woman was occupied in vigorously beating with a stick a strip of burning grass which had caught from the fire with which she had been cooking her evening meal. The boy ran to her assistance, and, thrusting her aside, lest her garments should become ignited, he began stamping the incipient blaze until he had succeeded in extinguishing it. The woman threw aside her stick and standing upright wiped her whole face indiscriminately with her bended arm.

"Damn him," she said, "I wish the whole thing had took fire and burnt up," and turning upon the boy, "did you see a man anywhere coming this way, leading a couple of mules?"

She was robust and young—twenty or thereabouts—and comely, in a certain rude, vigorous fashion. She wore a yellow-cotton handkerchief bound around her head somewhat in the manner of a turban.

Yes, the boy had seen a man watering two mules at the

trough before a road-house some distance away. He remembered it because the man was talking loud in some sort of a foreign, unfamiliar accent to a group of men standing by.

"That's him; damn him," she reiterated, and, moving towards the fire where she had been cooking; "want something to eat?" she asked, kindly enough.

The boy was not shocked at her language; he had not been brought up in "The Patch" for nothing. He only thought she had a more emphatic way of expressing herself than good manners or morals demanded. He did not swear himself; he had no positive leaning towards the emphatic, and moreover it was a custom not held in high esteem by Father Doran, whose teachings had not been wholly thrown away upon the boy.

Her offer of food was tempting and gratifying. A premonition that she was a woman who might take a first refusal as final, determined him to overcome all natural shyness and frankly accept without mincing.

"I'm mighty hungry," he admitted, turning with her towards the frying-pan and coffee-pot that rested upon the coals near the tent. She went inside and presently emerged bearing a brace of tin cups and a half loaf of bread. He had seated himself upon an inverted pine box; she gave him two slices of bread interlarded with bacon and a mug of coffee. Then, serving herself with the same homely fare, she sat down upon a second box and proceeded to eat her bread and bacon with great relish and to drain her cup of coffee.

It was quite dark now, save for the dim light of a road lamp nearby and the dull glow of the embers. The stars were coming out and the breeze was beating capriciously about the common, blowing the soiled canvas of the tent and buffeting a strip of cotton cambric that was loosely stretched between two poles at the edge of the road. The boy, looking up, remembered that he had read the inscription on the cambric, as he passed in the car: "The Egyptian Fortune Teller," in huge black letters on a yellow back-ground. It was fashioned to arrest the eye.

"Yes," said the woman, following his upward glance, "I'm a fortune-teller. Want your fortune told? But I don't talk like this here when I'm telling fortunes reg'lar. I talk a kind of Egyptian accent. That's his notion," motioning contemptuously with her head, down the road. "Because my skin's dark and my eyes, he goes to work and calls me 'The Egyptian Maid, the Wonder of the Orient.' I guess if my hair was yellow he'd call me 'The Swiss Fortune Teller,' or something like that and make me talk some kind of a *nicks-com-araus*. Only there's too many Dutch in this here country; they'd ketch on."

"You bet," said the boy.

The expression smacked of sympathy and reached her, some way. She looked up quickly and laughed. They both laughed. She had taken his cup from him and she was beating the two tins softly together, her arms resting on her knees.

"Where do you come from?" she asked with an awakened interest.

He told her he had come from Woodland Park, and how he had got there and why he was tramping it back to "The Patch." He even told her he was in no haste to regain "The Patch"; that it made no difference whether he ever got back or not; that he detested the crowded city and hoped soon to obtain employment in the country and stay there the rest of his life. These opinions and intentions took positive shape with him in the telling.

A notion or two got into her head as she listened to him. He seemed a companionable boy, though he was a good five years younger than herself. She thought of the long, slow journey ahead of her, the dreary road, the lonely hill-side, of those times in which her only human associate was a man who more than half the while was drunk and abusive.

"Come, go 'long with us," she said abruptly.

"Why?" he demanded. "What for? To do what?"

"Oh! there's lots of things you could do—help around, tell fortune maybe—'taint hard when you once get the hang of it, sell his old herbs and things when he's too drunk to talk. Why, lots o' things. Here, I ought to be pulling up stakes right now. Wait till you hear him when he comes back and finds I ain't done a thing! Hope I may die if I lay a finger to a stick of the measly truck," and she flung the tin cups, one after the other, into the open tent and maintained her careless, restful position on the soap box.

"Let me," offered the boy. "What you got to do? I'll do it." And he arose willingly, prompted by a decent feeling that he should do something in return for his supper.

"You can jerk them poles up and roll up the sign and stick it in the wagon; we're going to pull out of here in the morning. Then those pots and things got to be hooked under the wagon. Leave out the coffee pot."

While the boy busied himself in following her various instructions she talked on:

"I guess he's drunk down there—him and his mules! He thinks more of them mules than he does of me and the whole world put together. Because he paid two hundred and ten dollars for 'em he thinks they are made out o' some precious composition that's never been duplicated outside of Paradise. Oh! I'm about sick of playing second fiddle to a team of mules. Mr. Man'll wake up some o' these here mornings and find that I've cut an' run. Here! let that frying pan alone. He forgets I been used to better things than living in a tent. I sung in the chorus of an opera when I wasn't more than sixteen. Some people said if I'd had means to cultivate my voice I'd be—well, I wouldn't be here to-day, I can tell you."

The object of scorn and contumely was even then approaching; a short, broad-girted man, leading his sleek bay mules—splendid looking animals—and talking to them as he came along. In the dim light the boy could see that his hair, as well as his beard, was long, curly and greasy; that he wore a slouch felt hat over a knotted red handkerchief and small golden hoops in his ears. His dialect, when he spoke, was as indescribable as his origin was undiscernable. He might have been Egyptian, for aught the boy could guess, or Zulu—something foreign and bestial for all he knew.

The woman's name, originally Susan, had been changed to Suzima to meet the exigencies of her oriental character. The Beast pronounced it "Tzutzima."

"You can thank this here boy," she began by way of greeting. "If it hadn't been for him you wouldn't a found nothing here but a pile of ashes."

"So!" exclaimed the man in his greasy guttural, with utter lack of interest.

"Yes, 'so'! The whole blamed shooting-match was afire when he come along and put it out. If it hadn't been for him you wouldn't 'a found nothing here but a pile of ashes. He says he'll go along with us in the morning if we like. Looks like he knows how to work."

"That's good," agreed the man, "bring 'im along. Plenty of room where we live."

Usually "pulling up" time was one of contention between these two, each maintaining that the brunt of the work should be borne by the other. So the presence and timely services of the boy seemed to introduce a certain unlooked-for harmony into this unconventional *menage*. Suzima arose and went over to join the man, still occupied with the well-being of his mules.

He was smoking a short-stemmed pipe, which indicated that he had—wherever he got it—a sufficiency of food and drink, and would not trouble her on that score. They chatted pleasantly together.

When they retired into the tent for the night, the boy crept into the wagon, as he was instructed to do. It was broad and roomy and there he slept at ease the night through on a folded cotton "comforter."

## III

They wandered toward the south, idly, listlessly. The days were a gorgeous, golden processional, good and warm with sunshine, and languorous. There were ten, twelve, twenty such days when the earth, sky, wind and water, light and color and sun, and men's souls and their senses and the odor and breath of animals mingled and melted into the harmony of a joyful existence.

They wandered toward the south; the two vagabonds and the boy. He felt as if he had been transplanted into another sphere, into a native element from which he had all along been excluded. The sight of the country was beautiful to him and his whole being expanded in the space and splendor of it. He liked the scent of the earth and the dry, rotting leaves, the sound of snapping twigs and branches, and the shrill songs of birds. He liked the feel of the soft, springy turf beneath his feet when he walked, or of the rolling pebbles when he mounted a stony hillside.

Gutro, otherwise the Beast, drove his mules and talked to them, watered, washed and curried them; lavished upon them a care prompted by a wealth of affection and esteem. The boy was not permitted to touch the animals; he might not even think of them with their owner's knowledge or consent. But he had plenty else to do, with Suzima shifting the greater part of her work and duties upon him.

"I've got some time to sew now, thank heaven!" she said, and with a coarse thimble upon her clumsy finger and a needle threaded long, she sat at the back of the wagon or on a log in the warm air and constructed, with bits of cotton cloth, awkward-fashioned garments for the boy to wear next to his skin that she might wash those which he had on.

They moved along while the days were pleasant. Suzima must have felt glad as they went; for often-times, as she walked beside the slow-moving wagon through the still woods, she lifted her voice and sang. The boy thought he had never heard anything more beautiful than the full, free notes that came from her throat, filling the vast, woody temple with melody. It was always the same stately refrain from some remembered opera that she sang as she walked.

But on moonlight nights or when resting beside the camp fire, she brought forth a disabled guitar, and to a strumming accompaniment sang low, pleasant things, popular airs and little bits from the lighter operas. The boy sometimes joined her with his fluty girl voice, and it pleased her very well.

If Gutro was sober he took a degree of interest in the performance and made suggestions which proved that he was not devoid of a certain taste and rude knowledge of music.

But when Gutro was drunk, everyone, everything suffered but the mules. Suzima defied him and suffered the more for her defiance. She went about wincing and rubbing her shoulders and calling him vile names under her breath. But she would not let him beat the boy. She had a tender feeling for helpless and dependent things. She often exclaimed with impulsive pity over the dead and bleeding birds which they brought in from the forest. Gutro was teaching the boy to handle a gun, and many a tasty morsel they procured for their sylvan feasts. Sometimes they picked nuts like squirrels, gathering pecans when they reached the South country.

When it rained they sat bundled and huddled in the wagon under the streaming canopy, Gutro driving and swearing at the elements. Suzima was miserable when it rained and would not sing and would hardly talk. The boy was not unhappy. He peeped out at the water running in the ruts, and liked the sound of the beating rain on the canvas and the noise and crash of the storm in the forest.

"Look, Suzima! Look at the rain coming across the hill, yonder, in sheets! It'll be along here in three minutes."

"Maybe you like it," she would grumble. "I don't," and she would draw her shawl closer and crouch further in the wagon.

Often they traveled at night, when the moon shone; sometimes when it rained. They went creeping, the mules feeling their way cautiously, surely, through the darkness, along the unfamiliar roads. Suzima and the boy slept then in the bottom of the wagon on the folded "comforter." He often wished, at such times, that the wagon was broader or that Suzima would not take up so much room. Sometimes they quarreled about it, shoving, elbowing each other like children in a trundle bed. Gutro, in a rage, would turn and threaten to throw them both into the road and leave them there to perish.

## IV

The boy felt no little astonishment when he made Suzima's acquaintance in her official capacity of a fortune teller. It was a sunny afternoon and they had halted at the edge of a small country town and stopped there to rest, to make ready for a fresh start in the morning. Their presence created no little stir, and aroused some curiosity. Small children assembled and followed with absorbing interest the boy's activity in hoisting the sign, stretching the tent and setting forth the various and unique living utensils.

Gutro, robed in a long, loose robe of dingy scarlet and black, arranged, with much precision, upon an improvised table of boards, a quantity of vari-colored herbs and powders, unfailing remedies for any and every ailment which mankind had yet discovered or conceived. He was no faith healer, Gutro. He believed in the efficacy of things that grew, that could be seen and felt and tasted; green and bitter and yellow things. Some he had gathered at risk of life and limb on the steep ascents of the Himalayas. Others he had collected under the burning suns of Egypt; secret and mysterious, unknown save to himself and a little band of compatriots on the banks of the Nile. So he said. And the best of it, or the worst of it, was that those who listened believed and bought and felt secure in the possession of a panacea for their ailments.

Suzima, giving an extra twist to her yellow turban, sat at the door of the tent with a "lap-board," such as housewives use, extended across her knees. Upon this she laid out in bewildering array a pack of cards covered with pictures and mythical designs: a key, a ring, a letter or a coffin, a fine lady in a train and a finer gentleman on horseback. Suzima could tell fortunes by the cards or without the cards, off-hand, any way. The dialect which she assumed was not alone indescribable, but, for the most part, unintelligible, and required frequent interpretations from Gutro. There was no native Egyptian in that Southwest country to challenge her say and it passed muster and carried conviction. The boy could not withhold a feeling of admiration for her resources and powers of invention.

Suzima was over-blunt in her occult revelations to the negroes and farm-hands who loitered to learn somewhat of their destiny. But later, when youths and maidens from the village began to assemble and linger, half ashamed, wholly eager, then was Suzima all sentiment and sympathy, even delicacy. Oh! the beautiful fortunes that she told! How she lifted the veil of a golden future for each! For Suzima dealt not with the past. She would have scorned to have taken silver for telling anyone that which they already knew. She sent them away with confidence and a sweet agitation. One little maid sickened with apprehension when Suzima predicted for her a journey in the very near future. For the maid was even then planning a trip into Western Texas, and what might not this woman with the penetrating vision next foretell! Perhaps the appalling day and hour of her death.

Together Suzima and the boy sang their songs. It was the only part of the programme in which he took any part. He had refused to wear any foreign headgear or fantastic garb, or to twist his tongue into deceitful and misleading utterances. But he sang, standing behind Suzima bending over her guitar. There was more color in his face and lips now than when he had sat dreaming in Woodland Park. His eyes looked straight into the hazy distance, over the heads of the small gathering of people. Some of them looking at his upturned face, thought it was very beautiful. There was a tranquil light shining, glowing rather, from within; something which they saw without comprehending, as they saw the glow in the western sky.

At night, when everything was still, the boy walked abroad. He was not afraid of the night or of strange places and people. To step his foot out in the darkness, he did not know where, was like tempting the Unknown. Walking thus he felt as if he were alone and holding communion with something mysterious, greater than himself, that reached out from the far distance to touch him—something he called God. Whenever he had gone alone into the parish church at dusk and knelt before the red light of the tabernacle, he had known a feeling akin to this. The boy was not innocent or ignorant. He knew the ways of men and viewed them with tranquil indifference, as something external to which no impulse within him responded. His soul had passed through dark places untouched, just as his body was passing now, unharmed, through the night, where there were pitfalls into which his feet, some way, did not wander.

## V

Along in January the vagabonds felt that they would like to settle down for a time and lead a respectable existence, if only for the sake of novelty. Perhaps they would never have been so tempted if they had not stumbled upon a dismantled cabin pre-empted by a family of pigs whose ejection was but a matter of bluff and bluster joined to some physical persuasion. There was no door to the cabin, but there was part of a roof and a suggestion of chimney. And the wanderers were not over-exacting in their requirements, especially with no landlord at hand, to bow to his whims and fancies.

So they settled down to a domestic existence which some way proved to be not so united a one as their life on the road.

Near at hand was a big field where negroes were engaged during the day in clearing away stubble, some in plowing and others in bedding up cotton seed on the dry and unyielding parts.

Gutro, with the mules ever foremost in his mind, went out on the very first day and negotiated for their hire with the owner of the plantation, offering to throw himself in for *lagniappe*. A mule takes to the plow like the proverbial fish to water; then these were fine fellows with the brawn and muscle for freight hauling. When the planter took them for a month, Gutro followed and stuck to them and stayed by them. He sat on the wagon when they were driven to the landing. He kept his beady eyes upon them when they pulled the plow, and he was there at hand to note the quality and quantity of the provender dealt out to them. It would have been an evil hour for the negro who had dared, in his presence, to misuse or abuse one or the other of the animals.

Suzima and the boy went nosing about in search of bits of lumber with which to improve the condition of their temporary abode. But a stray plank was not easy to find, with everybody around patching fences, so they did not pursue their search with stubborn persistence, but went, instead, down the bank of the bayou and tried to catch some fish. The negroes told them that if they wanted fish they would have to go back to the lake; but they decided to drag crawfishes from the ditches along the field. The canvas-covered wagon marked them as "movers," and no one questioned or disturbed them.

That first night, when it came bedtime, they were unable to dispute the possession of the cabin with the fleas and, vanquished, they returned to the shelter of the tent. Next morning Suzima sent the boy to the village, a mile away, to learn, if possible, something about the disposition of that particular breed of fleas, and to acquaint himself with a method by which they might be induced to temper their aggressive activity.

It was Saturday. The boy discerned that there was a church in the village, and a pastor, who, arrayed in cassock, happened to be walking through his garden adjacent to the parsonage.

He went and spoke over the fence to the priest, who looked approachable, who was surely more approachable for him than would have been any other soul in that locality whom he might have encountered and addressed.

The priest was kind, sociable and communicative. He knew much about fleas, their habits and vices, and withheld nothing of enlightenment upon the subject from the boy. In turn he expressed some curiosity himself and a desire for information touching the particular stamp of young vagabond who had come sauntering along the road and who addressed him so cavalierly over his own fence. He was gratified to hear that the boy was a Catholic. He was astonished to discover that he could serve Mass, and amazed to hear that he liked to do so. What an anomaly! A boy who liked to serve Mass, who did not have to be coaxed, cajoled, almost lassoed and dragged in to do service at the Holy Sacrifice! And so he would be on hand betimes in the morning, would he? They parted friends, agreeably impressed, one with the other.

The boy was well pleased to find himself once more and so unexpectedly brought in touch with the religious life and the sacred office. As he traversed the road on his way back to the cabin he kept rehearsing the service half audibly.

"*Judica me, Deus, et discerna causam meam, de gente non sancta—ab homine iniquo et doloso erue me*"—and so forth.

He told Suzima he was going to the village to attend Mass the following morning.

"Go on," she said, "it won't hurt you. I've known people that were helped a sight by prayer-meeting. I'll go along too."

A part of her present scheme of respectability was a temporary discontinuance of the "Egyptian accent" and a suspension of professional performances. The yellow sign was not unfurled. She determined to contribute nothing during that restful month towards the household expenses. When she went into the village to church the following morning, with the boy, she had laid aside her yellow turban and wore a folded veil over her head. She looked not unlike some of the 'Cadian women who were there. But her carriage was freer and there was a vigorous vitality in her movements and in the gleam of her eyes that the milder 'Cadians did not possess. The little church, with its mixed congregation of whites and blacks interested her, and as she sat uncomfortably on the edge of the pew, her hands folded in her lap, she shifted her eyes constantly from one object to the other. But when the boy appeared with the priest before the altar, clad in his long white vestments, she was spell-bound with astonishment and admiration and her attention was not once again diverted from him. How tall he looked and how beautiful! He made her think of the picture of an angel. And when she saw him go through the maneuvers of serving with skill and ease, and heard his clear responses in a language which was not familiar to her, she was seized by a sudden respect and consideration which had not before entered into her feelings for him.

"Oh! it's out of sight!" she told him after Mass. "You got to wear one of them gowns on the road and talk that language: the Egyptian ain't in it."

"That's Latin," he said with a little bridling pride. "It only belongs in church, and I ain't going to talk it on the road for you or anybody. What's more, the vestments belong in church, too, and I wouldn't wear 'em outside to save my life. Why, it'd be a sin."

"A sin," marveled Suzima, who knew no delicate shades of distinction in the matter of sinfulness. "Oh pshaw! I didn't mean no harm."

They took their midday meal with the priest, who felt an interest in them and kindly offered them a share of his plain and wholesome fare. Suzima sat stiff and awkward at table, staring, for the most part, straight out of the open door, into the yard, where there were chickens scratching around and a little calf tied under a tree.

The boy feared for her own sake that she might forget herself and drop into the careless, emphatic speech which was habitual with her. But he need not have feared. Suzima spoke not at all, except in monosyllables, when she was politely addressed by the priest. She was plainly ill at ease. When the old gentleman arose to procure something from a side table, she winked at the boy and gave him a playful kick under the table. He returned the kick, not as a confederate, but a little viciously, as one who might say, "be quiet will you, and behave yourself in the company of your betters."

For a whole half day and more Suzima had been eminently respectable—almost too respectable for her own comfort. On their way back to the hut, as they passed a desolate strip of woodland, she gave a sudden impatient movement of the shoulders, as if to throw off some burden that had been weighing upon them, and lifting her voice she sang. There was even a ring of defiance in the vibrant notes. She sang the one stately refrain that had grown familiar to the boy and that he heard sometimes in his dreams.

"Oh!" he exclaimed impetuously. "I'd rather hear you sing than anything in the world, Suzima."

It was not often that she received words of admiration or praise and the boy's impulsive outburst touched her. She took hold of his hand and swung it as they went along.

"Say!" she called out to him that night, as she flung him his comforter, "it's good the Beast wasn't along. He don't know how to behave in company. He'd a' given the whole snap away, damn him."

## VI

Suzima's approval of the boy in sanctuary robes was explainable in view of the contrast offered by his appearance in everyday habiliments. She had done the best for his shabby garments with clumsy darns and patches. But what was her poor best, with himself doing the worst for them with broadening girth and limbs and hardening flesh and swelling muscles! There was no vestige of pallor now in his cheeks. Suzima often told him that he was not worth his salt, because his voice, which had been girlish and melodious, was no better now than the sound of a cracked pot. He was sometimes sensitive and did not like to be told such things. He tried to master the waverings and quaverings, but it was of no use, so he gave over joining Suzima in her songs.

The priest at the village did not mind so trifling a thing as the breaking of a boy's voice—a thing, moreover, which could not be helped—but he was concerned over the shabbiness and general misfit of his attire, and thereupon grew compassionate. He found employment for him in a store of the village and the boy, in exchange for his services, received a suit of clothes, taken down, brand new, from the shelf and folded in sharp creases. They were not of the best or finest, but they were adequate, covering his body completely and offering ample room for a fair play of limb and muscle.

He walked away each morning to the village, leaving Suzima alone, and he did not return till evening. His dinner he took at noon with the priest, and the two grew chatty and intimate over their soup. He confided to his venerable friend, when questioned, that he knew nothing of his companions of the road, absolutely nothing, except that they were Gutro and Suzima, who wandered across country in a covered wagon selling drugs and telling fortunes for a livelihood.

A shake of the head and a shrug of the shoulders can be very expressive and the boy read disapproval in these involuntary gestures of his old companion. Within his very own soul—that part of him which thought, compared, weighing considerations—there was also disapproval, but, some way, he was always glad to find Suzima sauntering down the road at evening to meet him. Walking beside her, he told her how his whole day had been spent, without reserve, as he would have spoken in the confessional.

"I don't know what the Beast's thinking about," she grumbled. "It's time to be pulling out of this here."

"I can't go till I'm through paying for my clothes," he told her determinedly.

"I got a few dollars that'll pay for these things," she told him. "They mighty poor stuff for the price, any way you look at it."

Poor stuff or not they had to be paid for, and this boy stood firm in his resolution to work out the balance due.

He brought religious newspapers and sometimes a book, which the priest gave him.

"What you want with them?" questioned Suzima, mistrustfully.

"Why, to read when I get a chance. A feller's got to read sometime, I guess." He put them carefully away in his pack, as he cared not to read by the flickering light of a candle or the uncertain flare of the brushwood in the dilapidated chimney. Suzima looked suspiciously upon these signs of ambition for enlightenment, especially as the papers and books were not of a character to entertain her. She examined them during the boy's absence.

One day she came to his encounter quite at the edge of the village, radiant, greeting him with a sounding slap on the shoulder. She was not so tall as the boy, but she felt he was an insignificant personage nevertheless, when not arrayed in canonicals, one whom she might patronize and with whom she might assume the liberty of equality and *camaraderie*, when so inclined.

"What you say? We going to pull out in the morning. He came back to-day with the mules. He made the devil of a noise when he didn't find you here to pack up, but I pitched in myself, and we got everything ready for an early start."

"Then I must go right back and tell them," said the boy, halting in the road.

"Don't need to tell nobody," she assured him. "You don't owe them nothing." The suit of clothes was, in fact, paid for and, moreover, he carried a small surplus in his pocket.

"No, but I got to go back," he insisted doggedly. He remembered quite distinctly—aside from Suzima reminding him of it—that he had not thought it essential "to go back" four months ago, when he decided to cast his lot with the wayfarers. But he was not now the child of four months ago. A sense of honor was overtaking him, with other manly qualities. He was quite determined to return to the village and bid good-bye to friends and acquaintances he had made there.

"Then I'll wait here," said Suzima, not too well pleased, seating herself on a low, grassy knoll at the edge of the road.

It was already getting dusk in the village. The store was closed, but the proprietor was still loitering near, and the boy went up and spoke to him and took his leave of him. He shook hands with an old gray-haired negro sitting on the porch, and bade good-bye to the children and boys of his own age who were standing about in groups.

The priest had just come in from his barnyard and smelled of the stable and cow. He met the boy on the gallery that was dim with the dying daylight filtering through the vines. Within, an old negress was lighting a lamp.

"I come to say good-bye," said the boy, removing his hat and extending his hand. "We going to start again in the morning." There was an excited ring in his voice that was noticeable.

"Going to start in the morning!" repeated the priest in his slow, careful, broken English. "Oh! no, you must not go."

The boy gave a start and withdrew his hand from the man's grasp, holding it thereafter to himself.

"I got to go," he said, making a motion to retire, "and it's getting kind of late now. I ought to be back."

"But, my friend, wait a moment," urged the priest, detaining him with a touch on the arm. "Sit down. Let us talk over it together." The boy seated himself reluctantly on the upper step of the gallery. He had too great reverence for the old man in his sacred character to refuse outright. But his thoughts were not here, nor was his heart, with the breath of Spring abroad beating softly in his face, and the odors of Spring assailing his senses.

"I got to go," he murmured, anticipating and forestalling his companion. Yet he could not but agree with him. Yes, he wanted to lead an upright, clean existence before God and man. To be sure he meant to settle down, some day, to a respectable employment that would offer him time and opportunity to gather instruction. He liked the village, the people, the life which he had led there. Above all he liked the man whose kindly spirit had been moved to speak and act in his behalf. But the stars were beginning to shine and he thought of the still nights in the forest. A savage instinct stirred within him and revolted against the will of this man who was seeking to detain him.

"I must go," he said again, rising resolutely. "I want to go."

"Then, if you must, God bless you and be with you, my son. Forget not your Creator in the days of your youth."

"No—no—never!"

"And bear in mind and in heart always the holy teachings of the church, my child."

"Oh, yes—always. Good-bye, sir; good-bye, and thank you, sir."

He had seen indistinctly the shadowy form of Suzima lurking nearby, waiting for him.

## VII

And now the wayfarers traveled northward following in the wake of Spring that turned to meet them radiant at every stage.

Many were the drugs and nostrums that Gutro sold as they went; for languor was on every side and people were running hither and thither with their complaints.

"It is the Spring," said the old people and the wise ones, with shrugs, as if to say: "The Spring is no great matter to worry over; it will pass." And then along came Gutro in the nick of time with powders that cleanse the blood and specifics that clear the brain, renew the "system" and reconstruct men and women, making them as it were perfect and whole.

When people are languid and tired they dream—what else can they do? Those day dreams that weave fantastic tricks with that time to come which belongs to them, which they can do with as they choose—in dreams! The young man rested at the plow and lost himself in thoughts of the superlatively fair one whom he had met the winter past in a distant county and whose image arose before him now to trouble him and to move him to devise ways to draw near to her. The maiden dropped the sewing from her hands to dream of she knew not what, and not knowing, it troubled her the more.

Then along came Suzima, the interpreter of dreams, with her mystic cards and Egyptian wisdom that penetrated and revealed.

The boy, on his side, was not idle. He knew the catch-penny trade; a job here and a helpful turn there that brought him small pieces of silver, which he always turned over to

Suzima. But he, too, had his dreaming time. His imagination was much stirred by the tales which Gutro told at night beside the camp fire. There was matter for speculation upon the amount of invention which entered into the telling of those personal experiences.

But what of that? It was the time when the realities of life clothe themselves in the garb of romance, when Nature's decoys are abroad; when the tempting bait is set and the golden-meshed net is cast for the unwary. What mattered if Gutro's tales were true or not? They were true enough for the season. Some of them left the boy not so tranquil. He began to remember and see, in a new, dawning light, things and people past.

He sometimes brought forth the books and papers which the priest had given him, and tried to read, lying flat on the grass, resting upon his elbows. But he could not find what he sought in the printed page, and he drowsed over it. The woods were full of lights and shades and alive with the flutter and songs of birds. The boy wandered about, for the most part alone, always moving on, restless, expectant, looking for that which lured and eluded him, which he could not overtake.

He would rather have dreamed or done anything that noonday than taken the mules to water. But here was Gutro, who was part human, after all, not wholly a beast, writhing in the clutch of twinges that have attacked more decent men than he. The fellow sat upon a stretched blanket beneath a tree, a huge leg extended, rendered helpless by a sharp and sudden pain which was well nigh unbearable. He could only sit and glare at the afflicted member and curse it.

"Try some of your own magic ointment," suggested the boy; then he turned and swore at the boy. And where was Suzima? Down at the pool, at the foot of the hill, washing the clothes. Oh! the wretch! Oh! the vile woman, to be washing clothes and he here with a hideous fate overtaking him, and the mules there, with lolling tongues, panting for water!

If the boy were not an idiot and a villain (and Gutro strongly suspected him of being both), he might be trusted to lead the valued animals to water. But he must have a care, a hundred cares, for that matter. One of the mules, he must remember, stumbled in going down hill; the other picked up loose stones in his hoof as he went. Then this one should not drink so much as he wanted, while the other should be urged to drink more than he seemed to want. The boy whistled a soft accompaniment to the litany of Gutro's instructions. He had no respect for the man and meant to tell him so some day. He walked away, leading the mules, meaning to deal with them as he saw fit, paying no attention whatever to the stumbling propensity or the instinct for picking up stones.

The air was heavy and hot as a day in summer. Not a leaf stirred on the branches above his head, and not a sound could be heard save the soft splash of the water down at the pool. He felt oppressed and unhappy; he did not know why, and his legs ached as he took long, slow strides down the grassy incline that led through a scattered wood to the water. He wondered what Suzima would say when she saw him for the first time intrusted to care for the mules.

She had finished her washing of the clothes. They were lying, wrung tight, in a small pile, on the pebbly bank. She was seated, naked, upon a broad, flat stone, washing herself, her feet in the water that reached almost up to her round, glistening knees.

He saw her as one sees an object in a flash from a dark sky—sharply, vividly. Her image, against the background of tender green, ate into his brain and into his flesh with the fixedness and intensity of white-hot iron.

"Oh! the devil!" she exclaimed, reaching back hurriedly for

the first garment that her hands fell upon, and drawing it across her shoulders. But she need not have troubled to cover herself. After that first flash, he did not look again. He kept his face turned from her, leading the mules to the water's edge, and staring down into the pool as they drank. There was no use to look at her; he held her as real and alive in his imagination as she was in the flesh, seated upon the stone.

She said not a word after the first impetuous exclamation. She did not go on with her ablutions, but sat drawn together, clutching the garment over her bosom and staring at him.

When the mules were satisfied he turned and led them up the hill again; but his every action was mechanical. There was a cold moisture on his forehead, and, involuntarily, he took off his hat and wiped his face with his shirt sleeve. His face, all his skin, to the very soles of his feet, was burning and pricking, and every pulse in his body was beating, clamoring, sounding in his ears like confused, distant drum-taps. He shook all over as he dragged his unwilling limbs up the ascent.

The sight of Gutro, bestial, seated helpless there upon the grass, seemed to turn the current of his passion in a new direction. He let the mules go and stood a moment, silent and quivering, before the man. It was only a moment's hesitation in which he seemed to be gathering all his forces to loosen in a torrent of invective and abuse. Where did the rage come from that maddened him? For the first time in his life he uttered oaths and curses that would have made Suzima herself quail. Gutro was suffocating; casting about for any object that his hands fell upon to hurl at the boy.

When the youth's senseless passion had spent itself, he stayed a moment, panting like a wounded animal, then, turning, fled into the woods. When he had gone far and deep into the forest, he threw himself down upon the ground and sobbed.

## VIII

Suzima treated the boy as she had never done before. She was less kind to him. She was cross and sulked for a time. It grieved him. He wanted to explain, to tell her that it was not his fault, but he did not dare to approach the subject, while she ignored it. Yet he felt that her ill-humor towards him was unreasonable. There was no renewal of his rage against Gutro, but he did not feel bound to apologize to that individual. Gutro doubted not that the boy was going mad and communicated his misgiving to Suzima. He related to her the scene which had transpired the day she was washing the clothes down at the pool, and intimated that it would be safe to get rid of so dangerous a character.

She had listened, scowling, but interested. Then she told Gutro a few uncomplimentary things on her own account.

The Beast was on his legs again. The pangs and twinges had gone as suddenly and mysteriously as they had come. But he was fearful of a second visitation, and determined to push on towards some point where he might procure professional and skillful treatment. Gutro was in no sense brave, nor was he foolhardy.

There came along some moonlight about that time and the vagabonds took advantage of it to travel by night.

It was the first night out; so beautiful, so still! The wagon moved along the white stony road, its white canopy gleaming in the white moonlight as it crept in and out of the shadows. The iron pots and pans hooked beneath the wagon swung to and fro with a monotonous, scraping sound.

Gutro sat huddled in a heap on the outside seat, half asleep as was his custom when he drove the mules at night. Suzima lay in the wagon and the youth walked on behind it. She, too, had walked some distance—not beside him as she used to, but more abreast of the wagon. She had been singing as she walked along and the echo of her song came back from a distant hillside. But getting tired at last she had sprung into the wagon and now she lay there. She had taken off her shoes and stockings and her bare feet peeped out, gleaming in the moonlight. The youth saw them and looked at them as he walked behind.

He wondered how long he could walk thus—if he could walk the night through. He would not go and sit beside Gutro; the physical repulsion which he felt for the man was too real to admit of such close contact. And there is a question whether Gutro would have permitted it, suspecting the boy, as he did, of being a dangerous and malicious character.

The boy walked on, stumbling. He was troubled, he was distracted and his breath failed him. He wanted sometimes to rush forward and take Suzima's feet between his hands, and then, on the other hand he wanted to turn and flee.

It was in response to neither of these impulses, but in submission to a sudden determination moving him, seemingly, without his volition, that he sprang into the wagon. He sat down at the back with his feet dangling.

The night was cool and pleasant. They were crawling along the edge of a hill, and the whole valley beneath spread out before them more soft, more radiant, more beautiful than brush could ever picture or voice ever tell. The boy did not know that it was pleasant and cool or that the valley was gleaming all for him in a magic splendor. He only knew that Suzima's bare feet were near him, touching him.

He supposed she was asleep. He drew himself up in the wagon and laid there beside her, rigid, faint, and quivering by turns. Suzima was not asleep. Turning, she folded her arms about him and drew him close to her. She held him fast with her arms and with her lips.

## IX

A few days had wrought great changes with the boy. That which he had known before he now comprehended, and with comprehension sympathy awoke. He seemed to have been brought in touch with the universe of men and all things that live. He cared more than ever for the creeping and crawling things, for the beautiful voiceless life that met him at every turn; in sky, in rock, in stream, in the trees and grass and flowers that silently unfolded the mysterious, inevitable existence.

But most of all he cared for Suzima. He talked and laughed and played with her. He watched her as she walked and turned about, and as she worked, helping her where he could. And when she sang her voice penetrated his whole being and seemed to complete the new and bewildering existence that had overtaken him.

There were a thousand new lights in Suzima's eyes that he watched for. She made pretty speeches that sounded in his ears as soft as the slow beating of the south wind. She had become something precious and apart from all things in the world and not to be confounded with them. She was the embodiment of desire and the fulfillment of life.

Suzima was defiant one day because Gutro was drunk. She was always defiant then—when he was brutal and nagging. The boy was near at hand, restless, quivering with apprehension of he knew not what. They had stopped to take their rude meal beneath the shade of a tree. Suzima and the boy were gathering up the utensils they had used. Gutro was hooking the mules to the wagon. He talked and nagged and Suzima talked and defied.

"Hush, Suzima," the boy kept whispering. "Oh, hush!"

Suddenly, the man, in a rage, turned to strike her with a halter that he held uplifted, but, quicker than he, the boy was ready with a pointed hunting knife that he seized from the ground.

It was only a scratch that he gave after all, for the woman had thrown herself against him with a force that diverted his deadly aim.

Gutro quaked and reeled with fright; he staggered and stood swaying, livid, with hanging jaw. Then, with a sudden revulsion of feeling that came with the dawn of illumination, he began to laugh. Oh, how he laughed! his oily, choking laugh! till the very woods resounded with the vile clamor of it. He leaned up against the wagon holding the fat cushion of his side and pointing a stub of finger. Suzima was red with consciousness, and scowling.

The boy said nothing, but sat down upon the grass. He was not red, like Suzima, but pale and bewildered. He lent no further hand in assisting their departure.

"Go on," he said, when they were ready to start.

"Come," said Suzima, making room for him in the wagon.

"Go on," he told her again. She thought that he would follow, taking a cut through the woods, as he often did. The wagon moved slowly away; the boy stayed leaning on his elbow, picking at the grass.

He had always supposed that he could live in the world a blameless life. He took no merit for he could not recognize within himself a propensity toward evil. He had never dreamed of a devil lurking unknown to him, in his blood, that would some day blind him, disable his will and direct his hands to deeds of violence. For he could not remember that he had willed. He knew that he had seen black and scarlet flashes before his eyes and he was conscious of an impulse which directed him to kill. He had as good as committed a crime for which they hang men. He stayed picking at the grass. An overwhelming confusion of thoughts, fears, intentions crowded upon him. He felt as if he had encountered some hideous being with whom he was not acquainted and who had said to him: "I am yourself." He shrank from trusting himself with this being alone. His soul turned toward the refuge of spiritual help, and he prayed to God and the saints and the Virgin Mary to save him and to direct him.

A mile or more back on the road they had passed an imposing structure built upon a hill. A gilded cross surmounted the pile. There were vineyards covering the slope, gardens and flowers and vegetables, highly and skillfully cultivated. The boy had noticed, when he passed, black-robed figures at work among the vines and in the meadow down along the fence.

The boy arose from the ground and walked away. He did not follow in the direction of the wagon. He turned and walked toward the building on the hill surmounted by a gilded cross.

## X

Brother Ludovic was so strong, so stalwart, that the boys of the institution often wished he might be permitted to give an exhibition of his prowess or to enter a contest of some sort whereby they might shine in the reflected honor of his achievements. Some said it all came of sleeping with open windows, winter and summer, because he could not abide the confinement of four walls. Others thought it came of chopping trees. For when he wielded his axe, which was twice the size of any other man's, the forest resounded with the blows. He was not one to dilly-dally about the grape vines or the flower beds, like a woman, mincing with a hoe. He had begun that way, they told each other, but he was soon away in the forest felling trees and out in the fields breaking the stubborn lands. So he had grown to be the young marvel of strength who now excited their youthful imaginations and commanded their respect. He had no mind for books, so they had heard—but what of that! He knew by name every bird and bush and tree, and all the rocks that are buried in the earth and all the soil that covered them. He was a friend of all the seasons and all the elements. He was a hero of the wood, to the vivid imagination of the young.

In reality he was still a youth, hardly past the age when men are permitted to have a voice and a will in the direction of government of the state. There was a stubborn growth of beard upon his face, which he shaved clean every morning and which wore the purple shadow again before night.

He often felt that he had been born anew, the day whereupon he had entered the gate of this holy refuge. That hideous, evil spectre of himself lurking outside, ready at any moment to claim him should he venture within its reach, was, for a long time, a menace to him. But he had come to dread it no longer, secure in the promise of peace which his present life held out to him.

The dreams of the youth found their object among the saintly and celestial beings presented to his imagination constantly, and to his pious contemplation. The bodily energy of youth spent itself in physical labor that taxed his endurance to the utmost. By day he worked, he studied, he assisted in the guidance and instruction of boys.

At night he slept a sleep of exhaustion, complete oblivion. Sometimes, at the approach of dawn, when his slumber lightened, some disturbing vision would weave itself into a dream to fool his fancy. Half asleep, half waking, he roamed the woods again, following, following, never overtaking a woman—that one woman he had known—who lured him.

"Come, come on!" she would say while the white-topped

wagon drew her always further and further away, out of his reach. But he knew a prayer—a dozen prayers—which could dispel any trick that a dream might put upon him.

## XI

Brother Ludovic had a great fancy, all his own, and one whose execution he was permitted to undertake. It was to build, with his own hands, a solid stone wall around the "Refuge." The idea had come to him like an inspiration, and it took hold of his imagination with the fixedness of a settled purpose in life. He was in a fever till he had begun his work: hauling the stones, laying them in position, binding them firm with sand and mortar. He liked to speculate upon the number of years that it would take him to complete the task. He liked to picture himself an old man, grown feeble with age, living upon this peaceful summit all enclosed by the solid stone wall built with the strength of his youth and manhood.

The Brothers were greatly interested and at the outset would collect together during the hours of recess, in small bands, and crossing vineyard and meadow, would repair to the scene of his labor.

"You'll not be telling me it's yourself that lifted the stone, Brother Ludovic?" and each would take turn in vain attempt to heave some monster which the younger man had laid in position. What would Brother Ludovic have done by the end of the year? was a never failing source of amiable controversy among them all. He worked on like the ant.

## XII

It was a spring day, just such another day as when he had first entered at the gate. The breeze lashed his gown about his legs as he quitted the group that had assembled after dinner to take their customary exercise around the brick-paved walk.

"It's a prison he'll be putting us in, with his stone wall!" called out a little jovial Brother in spectacles. Brother Ludovic laughed as he walked away, clutching at his hat. He descended the slope, taking long strides. So nearly perfect was his bodily condition that he was never conscious of the motion of limb or the movement of muscle that propelled him.

The wheat was already high in the meadow. He touched it with his finger-tips as he walked through, gathering up his narrow skirt as far as the knees. There were yellow butterflies floating on ahead, and grasshoppers sprang aside in noisy confusion.

He had obtained permission to work the whole afternoon and the prospect elated him. He often wondered whether it were really the work which he enjoyed or the opportunity to be out in the open air, close to the earth and the things growing thereon.

There was a good bit of wall well started. Brother Ludovic stood for a while contemplating with satisfaction the result of his labor; then he set to work with stone and mortar and trowel. There was ease in his every movement and energy in the steady glow of his dark eyes.

Suddenly Brother Ludovic stopped, lifting his head with the mute quivering attention of some animal in the forest, startled at the scent of approaching danger. What had come over him? Was there some invisible, malicious spirit abroad, that for pure wantonness had touched him, floating by, and transported him to other times and scenes? The air was hot and heavy, the leaves were motionless upon the trees. He was walking with aching limbs down a grassy incline, leading the mules to water. He could hear soft splashing at the pool. An image that had once been branded into his soul, that had grown faint and blurred, unfolded before his vision with the poignancy of life. Was he mad?

The moon was shining, and there was a valley that lay in peaceful slumber all bathed in its soft radiance. A white-topped wagon was creeping along a white, stony road, in and out of the shadows. An iron pot scraped as it swung beneath.

He knew now that he had pulses, for they were clamoring, and flesh, for it tingled and burned as if pricked with nettles.

He had heard the voice of a woman singing the catchy refrain from an opera; the voice and song that he heard sometimes in dreams, which vanished at the first holy exhortation. The sound was faint and distant, but it was approaching, coming nearer and nearer. The trowel fell from Brother Ludovic's hand and he leaned upon the wall and listened; not now like a frightened animal at the approach of danger.

The voice drew nearer and nearer; the woman drew nearer and nearer. She was coming; she was here. She was there, passing in the road beneath, leading by the bridle a horse attached to a small, light wagon. She was alone, walking with uplifted throat, singing her song.

He watched her as she passed. He sprang upon the bit of wall he had built and stood there, the breeze lashing his black frock. He was conscious of nothing in the world but the voice that was calling him and the cry of his own being that responded. Brother Ludovic bounded down from the wall and followed the voice of the woman.

"A Vocation and a Voice." Written November 1896. Published in Reedy's *Mirror* (St. Louis) (March 27, 1902).

# ELIZABETH STOCK'S ONE STORY

Elizabeth Stock, an unmarried woman of thirty-eight, died of consumption during the past winter at the St. Louis City Hospital. There were no unusually pathetic features attending her death. The physicians say she showed hope of rallying till placed in the incurable ward, when all courage seemed to leave her, and she relapsed into a silence that remained unbroken till the end.

In Stonelift, the village where Elizabeth Stock was born and raised, and where I happen to be sojourning this summer, they say she was much given over to scribbling. I was permitted to examine her desk, which was quite filled with scraps and bits of writing in bad prose and impossible verse. In the whole conglomerate mass, I discovered but the following pages which bore any semblance to a connected or consecutive narration.

* * *

Since I was a girl I always felt as if I would like to write stories. I never had that ambition to shine or make a name; first place because I knew what time and labor it meant to acquire a literary style. Second place, because whenever I wanted to write a story I never could think of a plot. Once I wrote about old Si' Shepard that got lost in the woods and never came back, and when I showed it to Uncle William he said: "Why, Elizabeth, I reckon you better stick to your dress making: this here ain't no story; everybody knows about old Si' Shepard."

No, the trouble was with plots. Whenever I tried to think of one, it always turned out to be something that some one else had thought about before me. But here back awhile, I heard of great inducements offered for an acceptable story, and I said to myself: "Elizabeth Stock, this is your chance. Now or never!" And I laid awake most a whole week; and walked about days in a kind of dream, turning and twisting things in my mind just like I often saw old ladies twisting quilt patches around to compose a design. I tried to think of a railroad story with a wreck, but couldn't. No more could I make a tale out of a murder, or money getting stolen, or even mistaken identity; for the story had to be original, entertaining, full of action and Goodness knows what all. It was no use. I gave it up. But now that I got my pen in my hand and sitting here kind of quiet and peaceful at the south window, and the breeze so soft carrying the autumn leaves along, I feel as I'd like to tell how I lost my position, mostly through my own negligence, I'll admit that.

My name is Elizabeth Stock. I'm thirty-eight years old and unmarried, and not afraid or ashamed to say it. Up to a few months ago I been postmistress of this village of Stonelift for six years, through one administration and a half—up to a few months ago.

Often seems like the village was most too small; so small

that people were bound to look into each other's lives, just like you see folks in crowded tenements looking into each other's windows. But I was born here in Stonelift and I got no serious complaints. I been pretty comfortable and contented most of my life. There ain't more than a hundred houses all told, if that, counting stores, churches, postoffice, and even Nathan Brightman's palatial mansion up on the hill. Looks like Stonelift wouldn't be anything without that.

He's away a good part of the time, and his family; but he's done a lot for this community, and they always appreciated it, too.

But I leave it to any one—to any woman especially, if it ain't human nature in a little place where everybody knows every one else, for the postmistress to glance at a postal card once in a while. She could hardly help it. And besides, seems like if a person had anything very particular and private to tell, they'd put it under a sealed envelope.

Anyway, the train was late that day. It was the breaking up of winter, or the beginning of spring; kind of betwixt and between; along in March. It was most night when the mail came in that ought have been along at 5:15. The Brightman girls had been down with their pony-cart, but had got tired waiting and had been gone more than an hour.

It was chill and dismal in the office. I had let the stove go out for fear of fire. I was cold and hungry and anxious to get home to my supper. I gave out everybody's mail that was waiting; and for the thousandth time told Vance Wallace there was nothing for him. He'll come and ask as regular as clock-work. I got that mail assorted and put aside in a hurry. There was no dilly dallying with postal cards, and how I ever come to give a second look at Nathan Brightman's postal, Heaven only knows!

It was from St. Louis, written with pencil in large characters and signed, "Collins," nothing else; just "Collins." It read:

"Dear Brightman: Be on hand tomorrow, Tuesday at 10. A.M. promptly. Important meeting of the board. Your own interest demands your presence. Whatever you do, don't fail. In haste, Collins."

I went to the door to see if there was anyone left standing around: but the night was so raw and chill, every last one of the loungers had disappeared. Vance Wallace would of been willing enough to hang about to see me home; but that was a thing I'd broken him of long ago. I locked things up and went on home, just ashivering as I went, it was that black and penetrating—worse than a downright freeze, I thought.

After I had had my supper and got comfortably fixed front of the fire, and glanced over the St. Louis paper and was just starting to read my seaside Library novel, I got thinking, somehow, about that postal card of Nath Brightman's. To a person that knew B. from hill's foot, it was just as plain as day that if that card laid on there in the office, Mr. Brightman would miss that important meeting in St. Louis in the morning. It wasn't anything to me, of course, except it made me uncomfortable and I couldn't rest or get my mind fixed on the story I was reading. Along about nine o'clock, I flung aside the book and says to myself:

"Elizabeth Stock, you a fool, and you know it." There ain't much use telling how I put on my rubbers and waterproof, covered the fire with ashes, took my umbrella and left the house.

I carried along the postoffice key and went on down and got out that postal card—in fact, all of the Brightman's mail—wasn't any use leaving part of it, and started for "the house on the hill" as we mostly call it. I don't believe anything could of induced me to go if I had known before hand what I was undertaking. It was drizzling and the rain kind of turned to ice when it struck the ground. If it hadn't been for the rubbers, I'd of taken more than one fall. As it was, I took one good and hard one on the footbridge. The wind was sweeping down so swiftly from the Northwest, looked like it carried me clean off my feet before I could clutch the handrail. I found out about that time that the stitches had come out of my old rubbers that I'd sewed about a month before, and letting the water in soaking my feet through and through. But I'd got more than good and started and I wouldn't think of turning around.

Nathan Brightman has got kind of steps cut along the side of the hill, going zig-zag. What you would call a gradual ascent, and making it easy to climb. That is to say, in good weather. But Lands! There wasn't anything easy that night, slipping back one step for every two; clutching at the frozen twigs along the path; and having to use my umbrella half the time for a walking stick; like a regular Alpine climber. And my heart would most stand still at the way the cedar trees moaned and whistled like doleful organ tones; and sometimes sighing deep and soft like dying souls in pain.

Then I was a fool for not putting on something warm underneath that mackintosh. I could of put on my knitted wool jacket just as easy as not. But the day had been so mild, it bamboozled us into thinking spring was here for good; especially when we were all looking and longing for it; and the orchards ready to bud, too.

But I forgot all the worry and unpleasantness of the walk when I saw how Nath Brightman took on over me bringing him that postal card. He made me sit down longside the fire and dry my feet, and kept saying:

"Why, Miss Elizabeth, it was exceedingly obliging of you; on such a night, too. Margaret, my dear"—that was his wife—"mix a good stiff toddy for Miss Elizabeth, and see that she drinks it."

I never could stand the taste or smell of alcohol. Uncle William says if I'd of had any sense and swallowed down that toddy like medicine, it might of saved the day.

Anyhow, Mr. Brightman had the girls scampering around getting his grip packed; one bringing his big top coat, another his muffler and umbrella; and at the same time here they were all three making up a list of a thousand and one things they wanted him to bring down from St. Louis.

Seems like he was ready in a jiffy, and by that time I was feeling sort of thawed out and I went along with him. It was a mighty big comfort to have him, too. He was as polite as could be, and kept saying:

"Mind out, Miss Elizabeth! Be careful here; slow now. My! but it's cold! Goodness knows what damage this won't do to the fruit trees." He walked to my very door with me, helping me along. Then he went on to the station. When the midnight express came tearing around the bend, rumbling like thunder and shaking the very house, I'd got my clothes changed and was drinking a hot cup of tea side the fire I'd started up. There was a lot of comfort knowing that Mr. Brightman had got aboard that train. Well, we all more or less selfish creatures in this world! I don't believe I'd of slept a wink that night if I'd of left that postal card lying in the office.

Uncle William will have it that this heavy cold all came of that walk; though he got to admit with me that this family been noted for weak lungs as far back as I ever heard of.

Anyway, I'd been sick on and off all spring; sometimes hardly able to stand on my feet when I'd drag myself down to that postoffice. When one morning, just like lightning out of a clear sky, here comes an official document from Washington, discharging me from my position as postmistress of Stonelift. I shook all over when I read it, just like I had a chill; and I felt sick at my stomach and my teeth chattered. No one was in the office when I opened that document except Vance Wallace, and I made him read it and I asked him what he made out it meant. Just like when you can't understand a thing because you don't want to. He says:

"You've lost your position, Lizabeth. That what it means; they've passed you up."

I took it away from him kind of dazed, and says:

"We got to see about it. We got to go see Uncle William; see what he says. Maybe it's a mistake."

"Uncle Sam don't make mistakes," said Vance. "We got to get up a petition in this here community; that's what I reckon we better do, and send it to the government."

Well, it don't seem like any use to dwell on this subject. The whole community was indignant, and pronounced it an outrage. They decided, in justice to me, I had to find out what I got that dismissal for. I kind of thought it was for my poor health, for I would of had to send in my resignation sooner or later, with these fevers and cough. But we got information it was for incompetence and negligence in office, through certain accusations of me reading postal cards and permitting people to help themselves to their own mail. Though I don't know as that ever happened except with Nathan Brightman always reaching over and saying:

"Don't disturb yourself, Miss Elizabeth," when I'd be sorting out letters and he could reach his mail in the box just as well as not.

But that's all over and done for. I been out of office two months now, on the 26th. There's a young man named Collins, got the position. He's the son of some wealthy, influential St. Louis man; a kind of delicate, poetical-natured young fellow that can't get along in business, and they used their influence to get him the position when it was vacant. They thinks it's the very place for him. I reckon 'tis. I hope in my soul he'll prosper. He's a quiet, nice-mannered young man. Some of the community thought of boycotting him. It was Vance Wallace started the notion. I told them they must be demented, and I up and told Vance Wallace he was a fool.

"I know I'm a fool, Lizabeth Stock," he said, "I always been a fool for hanging round you for the past twenty years."

The trouble with Vance is, he's got no intellect. I believe in my soul Uncle William's got more. Uncle William advised me to go up to St. Louis and get treated. I been up there. The doctor said, with this cough and short breath, if I know what's good for me I'll spend the winter in the South. But the truth is, I got no more money, or so little it don't count. Putting Danny to school and other things here lately, hasn't left me much to brag of. But I oughtn't be blamed about Danny; he's the only one of sister Martha's boys that seemed to me capable. And full of ambition to study as he was! It would have felt sinful of me, not to. Of course, I've taken him out, now I've lost my position. But I got him in with Filmore Green to learn the grocery trade, and maybe it's all for the best; who knows!

But indeed, indeed, I don't know what to do. Seems like I've come to the end of the rope. O! it's mighty pleasant here at this south window. The breeze is just as soft and warm as May, and the leaves look like birds flying. I'd like to sit right on here and forget every thing and go to sleep and never wake up. Maybe it's sinful to make that wish. After all, what I got to do is leave everything in the hands of Providence, and trust to luck.

"Elizabeth Stock's One Story." Written March 1898. First published in Per Seyersted, "Kate Chopin: An Important St. Louis Writer Reconsidered." *Missouri Historical Society Bulletin* (January 1963).

# TWO PORTRAITS (THE NUN AND THE WANTON)

## I
## The Wanton

Alberta having looked not very long into life, had not looked very far. She put out her hands to touch things that pleased her and her lips to kiss them. Her eyes were deep brown wells that were drinking, drinking impressions and treasuring them in her soul. They were mysterious eyes and love looked out of them.

Alberta was very fond of her mama who was really not her mama; and the beatings which alternated with the most amiable and generous indulgence, were soon forgotten by the little one, always hoping that there would never be another, as she dried her eyes.

She liked the ladies who petted her and praised her beauty, and the artists who painted it naked, and the student who held her upon his knee and fondled and kissed her while he taught her to read and spell.

There was a cruel beating about that one day, when her mama happened to be in the mood to think her too old for fondling. And the student had called her mama some very vile names in his wrath, and had asked the woman what else she expected.

There was nothing very fixed or stable about her expectations—whatever they were—as she had forgotten them the following day, and Alberta, consoled with a fantastic bracelet for her plump little arm and a shower of bonbons, installed herself again upon the student's knee. She liked nothing better, and in time was willing to take the beating if she might hold his attentions and her place in his affections and upon his knee.

Alberta cried very bitterly when he went away. The people about her seemed to be always coming and going. She had hardly the time to fix her affections upon the men and the women who came into her life before they were gone again.

Her mama died one day—very suddenly; a self-inflicted death, she heard the people say. Alberta grieved sorely, for she forgot the beatings and remembered only the outbursts of a torrid affection. But she really did not belong anywhere then, nor to anybody. And when a lady and gentleman took her to live with them, she went willingly as she would have gone anywhere, with any one. With them she met with more kindness and indulgence than she had ever known before in her life.

There were no more beatings; Alberta's body was too beautiful to be beaten—it was made for love. She knew that herself;

she had heard it since she had heard anything. But now she heard many things and learned many more. She did not lack for instruction in the wiles—the ways of stirring a man's desire and holding it. Yet she did not need instruction—the secret was in her blood and looked out of her passionate, wanton eyes and showed in every motion of her seductive body.

At seventeen she was woman enough, so she had a lover. But as for that, there did not seem to be much difference. Except that she had gold now—plenty of it with which to make herself appear more beautiful, and enough to fling with both hands into the laps of those who came whining and begging to her.

Alberta is a most beautiful woman, and she takes great care of her body, for she knows that it brings her love to squander and gold to squander.

Some one has whispered in her ear:

"Be cautious, Alberta. Save, save your gold. The years are passing. The days are coming when youth slips away, when you will stretch out your hands for money and for love in vain. And what will be left for you but—"

Alberta shrunk in horror before the pictured depths of hideous degradation that would be left for her. But she consoles herself with the thought that such need never be—with death and oblivion always within her reach.

Alberta is capricious. She gives her love only when and where she chooses. One or two men have died because of her withholding it. There is a smooth-faced boy now who teases her with his resistance; for Alberta does not know shame or reserve.

One day he seems to half-relent and another time he plays indifference, and she frets and she fumes and rages.

But he had best have a care; for since Alberta has added

much wine to her wantonness she is apt to be vixenish; and she carries a knife.

## II
## The Nun

Alberta having looked not very long into life, had not looked very far. She put out her hands to touch things that pleased her, and her lips to kiss them. Her eyes were deep brown wells that were drinking, drinking impressions and treasuring them in her soul. They were mysterious eyes and love looked out of them.

It was a very holy woman who first took Alberta by the hand. The thought of God alone dwelt in her mind, and his name and none other was on her lips.

When she showed Alberta the creeping insects, the blades of grass, the flowers and trees; the rain-drops falling from the clouds; the sky and the stars and the men and women moving on the earth, she taught her that it was God who had created all; that God was great, was good, was the Supreme Love.

And when Alberta would have put out her hands and her lips to touch the great and all-loving God, it was then the holy woman taught her that it is not with the hands and lips and eyes that we reach God, but with the soul; that the soul must be made perfect and the flesh subdued. And what is the soul but the inward thought? And this the child was taught to keep spotless—pure, and fit as far as a human soul can be, to hold intercourse with the all-wise and all-seeing God.

Her existence became a prayer. Evil things approached her not. The inherited sin of the blood must have been washed away at the baptismal font; for all the things of this world that she encountered—the pleasures, the trials and even temptations, but turned her gaze within, through her soul up to the fountain of all love and every beatitude.

When Alberta had reached the age when with other women the languor of love creeps into the veins and dreams begin, at such a period an overpowering impulse toward the purely spiritual possessed itself of her. She could no longer abide the sights, the sounds, the accidental happenings of life surrounding her, that tended but to disturb her contemplation of the heavenly existence.

It was then she went into the convent—the white convent on the hill that overlooks the river; the big convent whose long, dim corridors echo with the soft tread of a multitude of holy women; whose atmosphere of chastity, poverty and obedience penetrates to the soul through benumbed senses.

But of all the holy women in the white convent, there is none so saintly as Alberta. Any one will tell you that who knows them. Even her pious guide and counsellor does not equal her in sanctity. Because Alberta is endowed with the powerful gift of a great love that lifts her above common mortals, close to the invisible throne. Her ears seem to hear sounds that reach no other ears; and what her eyes see, only God and herself know. When the others are plunged in meditation, Alberta is steeped in an oblivious ecstasy. She kneels before the Blessed Sacrament with stiffened, tireless limbs; with absorbing eyes that drink in the holy mystery till it is a mystery no longer, but a real flood of celestial love deluging her soul. She does not hear the sound of bells nor the soft stir of disbanding numbers. She must be touched upon the shoulder; roused, awakened.

Alberta does not know that she is beautiful. If you were to tell her so she would not blush and utter gentle protest and reproof as might the others. She would only smile, as though beauty were a thing that concerned her not. But she is beautiful, with the glow of a holy passion in her dark eyes. Her face is thin and white, but illumined from within by a light which seems not of this world.

She does not walk upright; she could not, overpowered by the Divine Presence and the realization of her own nothingness. Her hands, slender and blue-veined, and her delicate fingers seem to have been fashioned by God to be clasped and uplifted in prayer.

It is said—not broadcast, it is only whispered—that Alberta sees visions. Oh, the beautiful visions! The first of them came to her when she was wrapped in suffering, in quivering contemplation of the bleeding and agonizing Christ. Oh, the dear God! Who loved her beyond the power of man to describe, to conceive. The God-Man, the Man-God, suffering, bleeding, dying for her, Alberta, a worm upon the earth; dying that she might be saved from sin and transplanted among the heavenly delights. Oh, if she might die for him in return! But she could only abandon herself to his mercy and his love. "Into thy hands, Oh Lord! Into thy hands!"

She pressed her lips upon the bleeding wounds and the Divine Blood transfigured her. The Virgin Mary enfolded her in her mantle. She could not describe in words the ecstasy; that taste of the Divine love which only the souls of the transplanted could endure in its awful and complete intensity. She, Alberta, had received this sign of Divine favor; this foretaste of heavenly bliss. For an hour she had swooned in rapture; she had lived in Christ. Oh, the beautiful visions!

The visions come often to Alberta now, refreshing and strengthening her soul; it is being talked about a little in whispers.

And it is said that certain afflicted persons have been helped by her prayers. And others having abounding faith, have been cured of bodily ailments by the touch of her beautiful hands.

"Two Portraits." Written August 4, 1895. Alternative title considered by Chopin: "The Nun and the Wanton." First published in Daniel Rankin's *Kate Chopin and her Creole Stories* (1932).

# AN IDLE FELLOW

I am tired. At the end of these years I am very tired. I have been studying in books the languages of the living and those we call dead. Early in the fresh morning I have studied in books, and throughout the day when the sun was shining; and at night when there were stars, I have lighted my oil-lamp and studied in books. Now my brain is weary and I want rest.

I shall sit here on the door-step beside my friend Paul. He is an idle fellow with folded hands. He laughs when I upbraid him, and bids me, with a motion, hold my peace. He is listening to a thrush's song that comes from the blur of yonder apple-tree. He tells me the thrush is singing a complaint. She wants her mate that was with her last blossom-time and builded a nest with her. She will have no other mate. She will call for him till she hears the notes of her beloved-one's song coming swiftly towards her across forest and field.

Paul is a strange fellow. He gazes idly at a billowy white cloud that rolls lazily over and over along the edge of the blue sky.

He turns away from me and the words with which I would instruct him, to drink deep the scent of the clover-field and the thick perfume from the rose-hedge.

We rise from the door-step and walk together down the gentle slope of the hill; past the apple-tree, and the rose-hedge; and along the border of the field where wheat is growing. We walk down to the foot of the gentle slope where women and men and children are living.

Paul is a strange fellow. He looks into the faces of people who pass us by. He tells me that in their eyes he reads the story of their souls. He knows men and women and the little children, and why they look this way and that way. He knows the reasons that turn them to and fro and cause them to go and come. I think I shall walk a space through the world with my friend Paul. He is very wise, he knows the language of God which I have not learned.

"An Idle Fellow." Written June 9, 1893. First published in *Complete Works of Kate Chopin* (1969).

# A MENTAL SUGGESTION

## I

"When you meet Pauline this morning she will be charming; she will be quite the most attractive woman in the room and the only one worthy of your attention and consideration."

This was the mental suggestion which Don Graham brought to bear upon his friend Faverham as the two were making their morning toilet together. Graham was a college professor, a hard working young fellow with a penchant for psychic research. He attended hypnotic seances and thereby had acquired a hypnotic power by no means trifling, which he sometimes exercised with marked success, especially upon his friend Faverham. When Faverham, getting up in the morning discovered that his black sack coat had assumed a vivid scarlet hue, he did not lament the fact or hesitate to put it on and present himself in public wearing so conspicuous a garment. He simply went to the telephone and rang up Graham:

"Hello! there—you blamed idiot! Stop monkeying with my coat!" Sometimes the message ran:

"Hello! This is the second morning I haven't been able to stand my bath—" or "here's my coffee spoiled again! By thunder! I want this thing to stop right here!" Whereupon a little group of professors at the other end of the "phone" would be moved by a current of gratification hardly to be understood by those who have never known the success of a scientific demonstration.

Faverham himself was not a hard worker. With plenty of money and a good deal of charm, he dispensed both lavishly and was a great favorite with both women and men. There was one privilege which he assumed at all times; he persistently avoided people, places and things which bored him. One being among others on earth who thoroughly bored Faverham, was Pauline, the fiancée of his friend Graham. Pauline was a brown little body with fluffy hair and eye glasses, possessed of an investigating turn of mind and much energy of manner in the pursuit of mental problems. She "went in" for art which she studied with a scientific spirit and acquired by mathematical tabulation. She was the type of woman that Faverham detested. Her mental poise was a rebuke to him; there was constant rebuff in her lack of the coquettish, the captivating, the feminine. He supposed she and Graham were born for each other and he could not help feeling sorry for his friend. Needless to say Faverham avoided Pauline and, so far as his instinctive courtesy permitted, snubbed her.

He and his friend were down at Cedar Branch where a number of pleasant and interesting people were spending the month of October.

On that particular October Monday morning, Graham was

returning to his engagements in the city and Faverham meant to stay on at the Branch so long as he could do so without being bored. There were a number of jolly, congenial girls who contributed somewhat to his entertainment, and beside the fishing was good; so were the bathing and driving.

As Graham stood before the mirror tying his cravat, the disturbing thought came to him that his little Pauline would have a dreary time during his two weeks' absence. With the exception of a German lady who collected butterflies and stuck pins through them, there was not a thoroughly congenial soul to keep her company. Graham thought of the driving, the sailing, the dancing in all of which Faverham was the leading and moving spirit and the temptation came to him to silently utter the suggestion which would convert Pauline from an object of indifference in Faverham's eyes to a captivating young woman. Under some pretext he approached and laid his hand upon Faverham who was lacing his boot. "When you meet Pauline this morning at breakfast she will be charming; she will be quite the most attractive woman in the room and the only one worthy of your attention and consideration."

There were a number of people assembled in the large dining room when Graham and Faverham entered. Some were already seated while others were standing chatting in small groups. Pauline was near a window reading a letter, absorbed in its contents which she hastened to communicate to her friend, after a hurried and absent-minded greeting. The letter was from an art-dealer, and all about a certain "example of Early Flemish" which he had obtained for her. Pauline was collecting facsimiles of the various "schools" and "periods" of painting with the precision and exactitude which characterized all her efforts. The acquisition of this bit of "Early Flemish" which she had been pursuing with unusual activity, settled her into a comfortable condition of mind.

Graham sat beside her and they brought their heads together and chatted psychology and art over their oatmeal. Faverham sat opposite. He kept looking at her. He was talking to the Tennis-Girl next to him and listening to Pauline.

"Miss Edmonds," he said abruptly, leaning forward so as to arrest her attention, "you must have Graham bring you around to my apartments when we're all in town again. I have a few pieces by the Glasgow men which I picked up last summer in Scotland and a bit of Persian tapestry that seems like a Hornel with the color toned down. Perhaps you would like to look at them."

Pauline flushed with surprise and pleasure. The Tennis-Girl drew back and stared at him. The Golf-Girl threw a pellet of bread at him from the far end of the table and Graham smiled and chuckled inwardly and took some mental notes.

Faverham maintained a lively conversation with Pauline across the table during the entire repast, while inwardly he was thinking:

"How wonderfully that soft brown suits her complexion and eyes! And what very sweet eyes she has behind those glasses. What depth! what animation! Could any thing be more captivating than that unstudied, spontaneous manner? and what a bright intelligence! By Jove! it puts a fellow on his mettle." Graham had reason to congratulate himself upon the success of his experiment.

Great was his astonishment however upon leaving table to see Faverham saunter away in company with the Tennis-Girl, evincing no particle of further interest in Pauline.

"How is this?" thinks Graham. "Ah-ha! to be sure! I suggested that he should think Pauline charming and captivating when he met her at breakfast. I must renew and qualify the suggestion."

When he went away, carrying his valise and things, Pauline

accompanied him to the gate which was a good stretch from the big, rambling house. He maintained a peculiar and rigid silence as they strolled down the gravel path that was already covered with fallen leaves. Pauline looked questioningly up at him.

"I wish, dear," he said, "you would abandon your thought to me; project all your mental energy into mine and let it follow and help the direction of my suggestion." The Golf-Girl might have doubted the sanity of such a speech; not Pauline; she was used to him. As he withdrew to go and shake hands with Faverham who was near-by, she converted her mind, so far as she was able, into a vacuous blank, abandoning it to his intention. The mental suggestion which Graham rapidly formulated as he held Faverham's hand, ran somewhat in this wise:

"Pauline is charming, intelligent, honest, sincere. She has depths in her nature that are worth sounding." He and the girl then walked silently together down to the gate and parted there with a mute pressure of hands.

He looked back as he went down the road. Pauline had turned and was regaining the house. Faverham had abandoned the tennis group and was crossing the lawn to join her. Graham took some fresh mental notes and patted himself metaphorically upon the back.

## II

In a letter which Pauline wrote a few days later to Graham, she said:

"I have not yet begun my notes on the Renaissance and I should have finished them by now! I deserve a scolding and hope you will not spare me. The truth is, I have been an idle girl and am quite ashamed of myself. You must have asked your friend Mr. Faverham to pay me a little attention. Were you afraid I should be bored? It was a misdirected kindness, dear, for he causes me to waste much time; he wanted to read Tennyson to me this morning out under the big maple when I had gone to begin those everlasting notes! I prevailed upon him to substitute Browning. I had to save something from this wreck of time! He is a delightful reader; his voice is mellow and withal intelligent, not merely musical. He was amazed at the beauty, the insight, the philosophy of our dear Browning. 'Where have you been?' I asked him in some surprise. 'Oh! in good company,' he avowed, 'but will you take me on a voyage of discovery and make me acquainted with the immortals?' But enough—If you have not yet seen Lilienthal about the Tintoretto" &c &c.

After a short interval she wrote:

"I am growing frivolous. I positively danced last night! You did not know I could dance? Oh! but I can; for I learned some pretty steps two winters ago when our 'Manners and Customs' class took up the history of dancing."

It was a week later that she said in a letter:

"I am distrustful of pleasures and emotions which reach one through other than intellectual channels. I received a singular impression a night or two ago. The evening was warm for October, and as there was a big, bright moon shining, Mr. Faverham, who had taken me for a sail, ventured to remain out longer than his usual hour for turning in. It was very late and very still. There was not a sound but the lapping of the little wavelets as the boat cut through the water, and the occasional flapping of the sail. The aromatic odor of the pines and firs wafted to us from the shore was very acute. I someway felt as if I were some other one, living in some other age and some other place. All that has heretofore made up the substance of my life seemed far away and unreal. All thought, ambition, energy had left me. I wanted to stay there forever upon the water, drifting, drifting along, not caring—I recognize that the whole experience was sensuous and therefore to be mistrusted."

Near the end of the two weeks there was a queer, rambling little note that seemed to Graham wholly out of character and irrelevant:

"You are staying away very long. I feel that I need you, to interpret me to myself if for nothing else. I fear there are forces in life against which the intellectual training makes no provision. Why are we placed at the mercy of emotions? What are the books for after all if we can snatch from them no weapons with which to meet and combat unsuspected and undreamed of subtleties of existence? Oh dear! Oh dear! Come back and help me disentangle it all." Graham was puzzled and uneasy.

## III

He returned to the Branch with the full intention of reclaiming his own. He was gratified with the success of his experiment, which at the same time had been the means of procuring for Pauline a period of diversion such as he believed would benefit her. His intention was to remove the suggestion he had put upon Faverham when everything would, of course, be as it was before.

If his love for the girl had been of the blind, passionate, exacting sort, perhaps he would have done so, even against the odds of changed conditions which met him.

"It may be a passing infatuation," she admitted with pathetic frankness. "I do not know; I have never felt anything like it before. If you wish—if you think it best and wisest to hold me to my promise you will find me ready to fulfill it. But as things are now, I must tell you that my whole temperament seems to have undergone a change. I—I sometimes—oh! I love him!"

She did not hide her face upon reaching the climax of her confession as most girls would have done, but looked out straight before her. They were sitting under the big maple where Faverham had read Browning to her; and the day was already beginning to fade. There was a light in her face that he had never seen there before; a glow such as he had never been able to kindle; whose source lay deeper in her soul than he had ever reached.

He took her small hand and stroked it quietly. His own hands were cold and moist. He said nothing except:

"You are quite free, dear; entirely free from any promise to me; don't bother; don't mind in the least." He might have said much more, but it did not seem to him worth while. He was letting go of things as he sat there so quietly: of some hopes, a few plans, pictures, intentions, and his whole being was undergoing the wrench of separation.

She said nothing. Love is selfish. She was tasting the exultation of liberty and shrank from inflicting the panacea of conventional phrase or utterance upon a wounded soul.

There were more things than one to trouble Graham. How had his suggestion held and how would it hold? There was no doubt that Faverham was still under the influence of the spell, as Graham detected at once upon first meeting him. The suggestion seemed to have got beyond the professor's control. He shuddered to think of the consequences; yet no course presented itself to him as acceptable but one of inactivity. There was nothing to do but hold off and let the experiment work itself out as it would.

Faverham said to him that night:

"I'm going away in the morning, old fellow. I'm a devilish nice sort of friend if you only knew it. Spare me the shame of explaining. When we meet again in town I hope I shall have pulled myself sufficiently together to understand a certain aberration of mind or morals—or—or—hang me if I know what I'm talking about!"

"I leave in the morning myself," returned Graham. "I may as well tell you that Pauline and I have discovered that we are not of that singleness of thought and that oneness of heart which offer the traditional pretext for two beings to cast their lots in common. We might go up to town together in the morning, if you like."

## IV

A few months later Faverham and Pauline were married. Their marriage seemed to mark the culmination of a certain tortuous doubt that possessed itself of the young professor and rendered his days intolerable. "If, if, if!" kept buzzing in his brain: during hours of work; while he walked or rested or read; even throughout the night when he slept.

He remembered Faverham's former dislike for the woman he had married. He realized that the aversion had been dispelled by means of a force whose limitations were as yet unknown; of whose possibilities he himself was wholly ignorant, and whose subtleties were beyond the control of his capacity. "How long will the suggestion hold?" This was the thought which preyed upon him. What if Faverham should awake some morning detesting the woman at his side! What if his infatuation should fade by degrees, imperceptibly; leaving her wrecked, stripped and shivering, to feed upon bitterness till the end of her days!

He visited them often during the first months of their marriage. People who knew them said their union was an ideal one; and for once, people were right. Unconscious impulses were tempering, acting, counteracting each other, inevitably working towards the moulding of these two into the ideal "one" of the poets' dreams.

Graham, when he was with them, watched them stealthily, with a certain cat-like intensity which, had they been less occupied with each other, they might have noticed and resented. It was always with a temporary relief he quitted them; a feeling of thankfulness that the lighted fuse had not yet reached the dynamite in the cellar.

But the torture of uncertainty became almost unbearable and once or twice he went to them with the full intention of removing the suggestion; to see what would happen, and have done with it. But the sight of their content, their mutual sympathy, palsied his resolution, and he left as he had gone to them, the prey of doubt and sharp uneasiness.

One day Graham reasoned it all out with himself. The state of worry in which he lived had become unbearable. He determined to that evening, remove the suggestion which he had fixed upon Faverham six months before. If he found that he could do so, then it would easily follow that he could again renew it, if he thought best. But if the disillusion had to come finally to Faverham, why not have it come now, at once, at the outset of their married life, before Pauline had too firmly taken the habit of loving and while he, Graham, might still hold enough of the old influence to offer a balm to her intellect and her imagination if not to her heart.

Graham, that night, realized more keenly than ever the change which Pauline had undergone. He looked at her often as they sat at table, unable to define what was yet so apparent. She was a pretty woman now. There was color in her face whose contour was softened and embellished by a peculiarly happy arrangement of her brown hair. The pince-nez which she had substituted for the rather formidable spectacles, while depriving her face somewhat of its former student-air, lent it a piquancy that was very attractive. Her gown was rich as her husband's purse could buy and its colors were marvelously soft, indefinable, harmonious, making of the garment a distinct part of herself and her surroundings.

Graham seemed to take his place and fit into this small ménage as an essential and valued part of it. He certainly felt in no trifling degree responsible for its existence. That night he felt like some patriarch of old about to immolate a cherished object upon the altar of science—a victim to the insatiable God of the Inevitable.

It was not during that pleasant moment of dining, but later in the evening that Graham chose to tempt once more the power which he had played with and which, like some venomous, unknown reptile had stung and wounded him.

They sat drowsily before the remnant of a wood-fire that had spent itself, and glowed now, and flamed fitfully. Faverham had been reading aloud by the light of a single lamp, soft lines whose beauty had melted and entered into their souls like an ointment, soothing them to inward contemplation rather than moving them to speech and wordy discussion. The book yet hung from his hand as he stared into the glow of embers. There was a flurry of rain beating against the window panes. Graham, buried in the cushioned depths of an armchair, gazed at Faverham. Pauline had arisen and she walked slowly to and fro in the apartment, her garments making a soft, pleasant rustle as she moved in and out of the shadows. Graham felt that the moment had come.

He arose and went towards the lamp to light the cigar which he took from his pocket. As he stood beside the table he rested a hand carelessly upon the shoulder of his friend.

"Pauline is the woman she was six months ago. She is not charming or attractive," he suggested silently. "Pauline is the woman she was six months ago when she first went to Cedar Branch." Graham lit his cigar at the lamp and returned to his chair in the shadow.

Faverham shivered as if a cold breath had swept by him, and drew his lounge a little nearer the fire. He turned his head and looked at his wife as she passed in her slow walk. Again he gazed into the fire, then restlessly back at his wife; over and over. Graham kept his eyes fixed upon him, silently repeating the suggestion.

Suddenly Faverham arose, letting the book fall unnoticed to the floor. Impetuously he approached his wife and taking her in his arms as if he had been alone with her, he held her close, while passionately, almost rudely, he kissed her flushed and startled face, over and over, hungrily. She was panting, and red with confusion and annoyance when he finally released her from his ardent embrace.

"Polly, Polly!" he entreated, "forgive me," for she went and hid her face in the cushion of a chair; "don't mind, dearest. Graham knows how much I love you." He turned and walked towards the fire. He was agitated and passed his hand in an unmeaning fashion across his forehead.

"I don't know when I've made such an ass of myself," he said apologetically in a low tone to Graham. "I hope you'll forgive the tactless display of emotion. The truth is, I feel hardly responsible for it myself; more as if I had obeyed some imperative impulse driving me to an emphatic expression. I admit it was ill-timed," he laughed; "over-mastering love is my only excuse."

Graham did not stay much longer. A sense of relief—release—was overpowering him. But he was baffled; he wanted to be alone to puzzle the phenomenon out according to his lights.

He did not lift his umbrella, but rather welcomed the dash

of rain in his face as he strode along the glistening pavement. There was a good bit of a walk before him and it was only towards the end of it, when the rain had stopped and a few little stars were blinking down at him, that the truth finally dawned. He remembered that six months ago he had suggested to Faverham that Pauline was charming, captivating, intelligent, honest, worthy of study. But what about love? He had said nothing of that. Love had come unbidden, without a "will you?" or a "by your leave"; and there was love in possession, holding his own against any power of the universe. It was indeed a great illumination to Graham.

He gave rein to his imagination. Recalling Faverham's singular actions under the last hypnotic suggestion, he hugged the fancy that the two forces, love, and the imperative suggestion had waged a short, fierce conflict within the man's subconsciousness, and love had triumphed. He positively believed this.

Graham looked up at the little winking stars and they looked down at him. He bowed in acknowledgment to the supremacy of the moving power which is love; which is life.

"A Mental Suggestion." Written December 1896. First published in *Complete Works of Kate Chopin* (1969).

# AN EGYPTIAN CIGARETTE

My friend, the Architect, who is something of a traveler, was showing us various curios which he had gathered during a visit to the Orient.

"Here is something for you," he said, picking up a small box and turning it over in his hand. "You are a cigarette-smoker; take this home with you. It was given to me in Cairo by a species of fakir, who fancied I had done him a good turn."

The box was covered with glazed, yellow paper, so skillfully gummed as to appear to be all one piece. It bore no label, no stamp—nothing to indicate its contents.

"How do you know they are cigarettes?" I asked, taking the box and turning it stupidly around as one turns a sealed letter and speculates before opening it.

"I only know what he told me," replied the Architect, "but it is easy enough to determine the question of his integrity."

He handed me a sharp, pointed paper-cutter, and with it I opened the lid as carefully as possible.

The box contained six cigarettes, evidently hand-made. The wrappers were of pale-yellow paper, and the tobacco was almost the same color. It was of finer cut than the Turkish or ordinary Egyptian, and threads of it stuck out at either end.

"Will you try one now, Madam?" asked the Architect, offering to strike a match.

"Not now and not here," I replied, "after the coffee, if you will permit me to slip into your smoking-den. Some of the women here detest the odor of cigarettes."

The smoking-room lay at the end of a short, curved passage. Its appointments were exclusively oriental. A broad, low window opened out upon a balcony that overhung the garden. From the divan upon which I reclined, only the swaying tree-tops could be seen. The maple leaves glistened in the afternoon sun. Beside the divan was a low stand which contained the complete paraphernalia of a smoker. I was feeling quite comfortable, and congratulated myself upon having escaped for a while the incessant chatter of the women that reached me faintly.

I took a cigarette and lit it, placing the box upon the stand just as the tiny clock, which was there, chimed in silvery strokes the hour of five.

I took one long inspiration of the Egyptian cigarette. The gray-green smoke arose in a small puffy column that spread and broadened, that seemed to fill the room. I could see the maple leaves dimly, as if they were veiled in a shimmer of moonlight. A subtle, disturbing current passed through my whole body and went to my head like the fumes of disturbing wine. I took another deep inhalation of the cigarette.

* * *

"Ah! the sand has blistered my cheek! I have lain here all day with my face in the sand. Tonight, when the everlasting stars are burning, I shall drag myself to the river."

He will never come back.

Thus far I followed him; with flying feet; with stumbling feet; with hands and knees, crawling; and outstretched arms, and here I have fallen in the sand.

The sand has blistered my cheek; it has blistered all my body, and the sun is crushing me with hot torture. There is shade beneath yonder cluster of palms.

I shall stay here in the sand till the hour and the night comes.

I laughed at the oracles and scoffed at the stars when they told that after the rapture of life I would open my arms inviting death, and the waters would envelop me.

Oh! how the sand blisters my cheek! and I have no tears to quench the fire. The river is cool and the night is not far distant.

I turned from the gods and said: "There is but one; Bardja is my god." That was when I decked myself with lilies and wove flowers into a garland and held him close in the frail, sweet fetters.

He will never come back. He turned upon his camel as he rode away. He turned and looked at me crouching here and laughed, showing his gleaming white teeth.

Whenever he kissed me and went away he always came back again. Whenever he flamed with fierce anger and left me with stinging words, he always came back. But to-day he neither kissed me nor was he angry. He only said:

"Oh! I am tired of fetters, and kisses, and you. I am going away. You will never see me again. I am going to the great city where men swarm like bees. I am going beyond, where the monster stones are rising heavenward in a monument for the unborn ages. Oh! I am tired. You will see me no more."

And he rode away on his camel. He smiled and showed his cruel white teeth as he turned to look at me crouching here.

How slow the hours drag! It seems to me that I have lain here for days in the sand, feeding upon despair. Despair is bitter and it nourishes resolve.

I hear the wings of a bird flapping above my head, flying low, in circles.

The sun is gone.

The sand has crept between my lips and teeth and under my parched tongue.

If I raise my head, perhaps I shall see the evening star.

Oh! the pain in my arms and legs! My body is sore and bruised as if broken. Why can I not rise and run as I did this morning? Why must I drag myself thus like a wounded serpent, twisting and writhing?

The river is near at hand. I hear it—I see it—Oh! the sand! Oh! the shine! How cool! how cold!

The water! the water! In my eyes, my ears, my throat! It strangles me! Help! will the gods not help me?

Oh! the sweet rapture of rest! There is music in the Temple. And here is fruit to taste. Bardja came with the music—The moon shines and the breeze is soft—A garland of flowers—let us go into the King's garden and look at the blue lily, Bardja.

The maple leaves looked as if a silvery shimmer enveloped them. The gray-green smoke no longer filled the room. I could hardly lift the lids of my eyes. The weight of centuries seemed to suffocate my soul that struggled to escape, to free itself and breathe.

I had tasted the depths of human despair.

The little clock upon the stand pointed to a quarter past five. The cigarettes still reposed in the yellow box. Only the stub of the one I had smoked remained. I had laid it in the ash tray.

As I looked at the cigarettes in their pale wrappers, I wondered what other visions they might hold for me; what might I not find in their mystic fumes? Perhaps a vision of celestial peace; a dream of hopes fulfilled; a taste of rapture, such as had not entered into my mind to conceive.

I took the cigarettes and crumpled them between my hands. I walked to the window and spread my palms wide. The light breeze caught up the golden threads and bore them writhing and dancing far out among the maple leaves.

My friend, the Architect, lifted the curtain and entered, bringing me a second cup of coffee.

"How pale you are!" he exclaimed, solicitously. "Are you not feeling well?"

"A little the worse for a dream," I told him.

"An Egyptian Cigarette." Written April 1897. Published in *Vogue* (April 19, 1900).

# THE WHITE EAGLE

It was not an eagle of flesh and feathers but a cast-iron bird poised with extended wings and wearing an expression which, in a human being, would have passed for wisdom. He stood conspicuously upon the lawn of an old homestead. In the spring, if any white paint went the rounds, he came in for his share of it, otherwise he had to be content with a coat of whitewash such as the sheds and fences were treated to.

But he was always proud; in the summer standing spotless on the green with a background of climbing roses; when the leaves fell softly and he began to show unsightly spots here and there; when the snow wrapped him like a shroud, or the rain beat upon him and the wind struck at him with wild fury—he was always proud.

A small child could sit in the shadow of his wings. There was one who often did on sunny days while her soul drank the unconscious impressions of childhood. Later she grew sensible of her devotion for the white eagle and she often caressed his venerable head or stroked his wings in passing on the lawn.

But people die and children squabble over estates, large or small. This estate was not large, but the family was, and it seemed but a pittance that fell to the share of each. The girl secured her portion and the white eagle beside; no one else wanted it. She moved her belongings up the street into a pleasant room of a neighbor who rented lodgings. The eagle was set down in the back yard under an apple tree, and for a while he succeeded in keeping the birds away. But they grew accustomed to his brooding presence and often alighted on his outspread wings after their mischievous onslaughts upon the apples. Indeed he seemed to be of no earthly use except to have sheltered the unconscious summer dreams of a small child.

People wondered at the young woman's persistence in carting him about with her when she moved from place to place. Her want of perspicacity might have explained this eccentricity. It explained many other things, chiefly the misfortune which overtook her of losing her small share of the small estate. But that is such an ordinary human experience, it seems useless to mention it; and, besides, the white eagle had nothing to do with it.

There was finally no place for him save in a corner of her narrow room, that was otherwise crowded with a bed, a chair or two, a table and a sewing machine, that always stood by the window. Oftentimes when she sewed at the machine, or else from her bed before she arose in the early dawn, she fancied the white eagle blinked at her from his sombre corner on the floor, an effect produced by remnants of white paint that still stuck in his deep eye sockets.

The years went by, slowly, swiftly, haltingly as they marked off the uneven progress of her life. No mate came to seek her out. Her hair began to grizzle. Her skin got dry and waxlike upon her face and hands. Her chest grew shrunken from eternal bending over the sewing machine and lack of pure, fresh air. The white eagle was always there in the gloomy corner. He helped her to remember; or, better, he never permitted her to forget. Sometimes little children in the house penetrated to her room, and amused themselves with him. Once they made a Christmas spectacle of him with a cocked hat and bits of tawdry tinsel suspended from his wings.

When the woman—no longer young—grew sick and had a fierce fever, she uttered a shriek in the night which brought a straggler inquiring at her bedside. The eagle had blinked and blinked, had left his corner and come and perched upon her, pecking at her bosom. That was the last she knew of her white eagle in this life. She died, and a close relative, with some sentiment and possessing the means of transportation, came from a distance and laid her out suitably and buried her decently in the old cemetery on the side of the hill. It was far up on the very crest, overlooking a vast plain that reached out to the horizon.

None of her belongings, save perhaps the sewing machine, were of a character to arouse family interest. No one knew what to do with the white eagle. The suggestion that it be thrown into the ash-bin was not favorably received by the sentimental relative, who happened to remember a small, barefooted child seated in the summer grass within the shadow of its outstretched wings.

So the white eagle was carted for the last time up the hill to the old cemetery and placed like a tombstone at the head of her grave. He has stood there for years. Sometimes little children in spring throw wreaths of clover-blossoms over him. The blossoms dry and rot and fall to pieces in time. The grave has sunk unkept to the level. The grass grows high above it in the summer time. With the sinking grave the white eagle has dipped forward as if about to take his flight. But he never does. He gazes across the vast plain with an expression which in a human being would pass for wisdom.

"The White Eagle." Written May 9, 1900. Published in *Vogue* (July 12, 1900).

# THE STORY OF AN HOUR (THE DREAM OF AN HOUR)

Knowing that Mrs. Mallard was afflicted with a heart trouble, great care was taken to break to her as gently as possible the news of her husband's death.

It was her sister Josephine who told her, in broken sentences; veiled hints that revealed in half concealing. Her husband's friend Richards was there, too, near her. It was he who had been in the newspaper office when intelligence of the railroad disaster was received, with Brently Mallard's name leading the list of "killed." He had only taken the time to assure himself of its truth by a second telegram, and had hastened to forestall any less careful, less tender friend in bearing the sad message.

She did not hear the story as many women have heard the same, with a paralyzed inability to accept its significance. She wept at once, with sudden, wild abandonment, in her sister's arms. When the storm of grief had spent itself she went away to her room alone. She would have no one follow her.

There stood, facing the open window, a comfortable, roomy armchair. Into this she sank, pressed down by a physical exhaustion that haunted her body and seemed to reach into her soul.

She could see in the open square before her house the tops of trees that were all aquiver with the new spring life. The delicious breath of rain was in the air. In the street below a peddler was crying his wares. The notes of a distant song which some one was singing reached her faintly, and countless sparrows were twittering in the eaves.

There were patches of blue sky showing here and there through the clouds that had met and piled one above the other in the west facing her window.

She sat with her head thrown back upon the cushion of the chair, quite motionless, except when a sob came up into her throat and shook her, as a child who has cried itself to sleep continues to sob in its dreams.

She was young, with a fair, calm face, whose lines bespoke repression and even a certain strength. But now there was a dull stare in her eyes, whose gaze was fixed away off yonder on one of those patches of blue sky. It was not a glance of reflection, but rather indicated a suspension of intelligent thought.

There was something coming to her and she was waiting for it, fearfully. What was it? She did not know; it was too subtle and elusive to name. But she felt it, creeping out of the sky, reaching toward her through the sounds, the scents, the color that filled the air.

Now her bosom rose and fell tumultuously. She was beginning to recognize this thing that was approaching to possess her, and she was striving to beat it back with her will—as powerless as her two white slender hands would have been.

When she abandoned herself a little whispered word escaped her slightly parted lips. She said it over and over under her breath: "free, free, free!" The vacant stare and the look of terror that had followed it went from her eyes. They stayed keen and bright. Her pulses beat fast, and the coursing blood warmed and relaxed every inch of her body.

She did not stop to ask if it were or were not a monstrous joy that held her. A clear and exalted perception enabled her to dismiss the suggestion as trivial.

She knew that she would weep again when she saw the kind, tender hands folded in death; the face that had never looked save with love upon her, fixed and gray and dead. But she saw beyond that bitter moment a long procession of years to come that would belong to her absolutely. And she opened and spread her arms out to them in welcome.

There would be no one to live for her during those coming years; she would live for herself. There would be no powerful will bending hers in that blind persistence with which men and women believe they have a right to impose a private will upon a fellow-creature. A kind intention or a cruel intention made the act seem no less a crime as she looked upon it in that brief moment of illumination.

And yet she had loved him—sometimes. Often she had not. What did it matter! What could love, the unsolved mystery, count for in face of this possession of self-assertion which she suddenly recognized as the strongest impulse of her being!

"Free! Body and soul free!" she kept whispering.

Josephine was kneeling before the closed door with her lips to the keyhole, imploring for admission. "Louise, open the door! I beg; open the door—you will make yourself ill. What are you doing, Louise? For heaven's sake open the door."

"Go away. I am not making myself ill." No; she was drinking in a very elixir of life through that open window.

Her fancy was running riot along those days ahead of her. Spring days, and summer days, and all sorts of days that would be her own. She breathed a quick prayer that life might be long. It was only yesterday she had thought with a shudder that life might be long.

She arose at length and opened the door to her sister's importunities. There was a feverish triumph in her eyes, and she carried herself unwittingly like a goddess of Victory. She clasped her sister's waist, and together they descended the stairs. Richards stood waiting for them at the bottom.

Some one was opening the front door with a latchkey. It was Brently Mallard who entered, a little travel-stained, composedly carrying his grip-sack and umbrella. He had been far from the scene of accident, and did not even know there had been one. He stood amazed at Josephine's piercing cry; at Richards' quick motion to screen him from the view of his wife.

But Richards was too late.

When the doctors came they said she had died of heart disease—of joy that kills.

"The Dream of an Hour." Written April 19, 1894. Published in *Vogue* (December 6, 1894). Later called "The Story of an Hour."

# TWO SUMMERS AND TWO SOULS

## I

He was a fine, honest-looking fellow; young, impetuous, candid; and he was bidding her good-bye.

It was in the country, where she lived, and where her soul and senses were slowly unfolding, like the languid petals of some white and fragrant blossom.

Five weeks—only five weeks he had known her. They seemed to him a flash, an eternity, a rapturous breath, an existence—a re-creation of light and life, and soul and senses. He tried to tell her something of this when the hour of parting came. But he could only say that he loved her; nothing else that he wanted to say seemed to mean so much as this. She was glad, and doubtful, and afraid, and kept reiterating:

"Only five weeks! so short! and love and life are so long."

"Then you don't love me!"

"I don't know. I want to be with you—near you."

"Then you do love me!"

"I don't know. I thought love meant something different—powerful, overwhelming. No. I am afraid to say."

He talked like a mad man then, and troubled and bewildered her with his incoherence. He begged for love as a mendicant might beg for alms, without reserve and without shame, and the passion within him gave an unnatural ring to his voice and a new, strange look to his eyes that chilled her unawakened senses and sent her shivering within herself.

"No, no, no!" was all she could say to him.

He willed not to believe it; he had felt so sure of her. And she was not one to play fast and loose, with those honest eyes whose depths had convinced while they ensnared him.

"Don't send me away like this," he pleaded, "without a crumb of hope to feed on and keep me living."

She dismissed him with a promise that it might not be final. "Who knows! I will think; but leave me alone. Don't trouble me; and I will see—Good-bye."

He did not once look back after leaving her, but walked straight on with a step that was quick and firm from habit. But he was almost blind and senseless from pain.

She stayed watching him cross the lawn and the long stretch of meadow beyond. She watched him till the deepening shadows of the coming night crept between them. She stayed troubled, uncertain; tearful because she did not know!

## II

"I remember quite well the words I told you a year ago when we parted," she wrote to him. "I told you I did not know, I wanted to think, I even wanted to pray, but I believe I did not tell you that. And now, will you believe me when I say that I have not been able to think—hardly to pray. I have only been able to feel. When you went away that day you seemed to leave me in an empty world. I kept saying to myself, 'to-morrow or next day it will be different; it will be with me as it was before he came.' Then your letters coming—three of them, one upon the other—gave voice to the empty places. You were everywhere after that. And still I doubted, and I was cautious; for it has seemed to me that the love which is to hold two beings together through life must be love indeed.

"But what is the use of saying more than that I love you. I would not care to live without you; I think I could not. Come back to me."

## III

When this letter reached him he was in preparation for a journey with a party of friends. It came with a batch of business letters, and in the midst of the city's rush and din which he had meant in another day to leave behind him.

He was all unprepared for its coming and unable at once to master the shock of it, that bewildered and unnerved him.

Then came back to him the recollection of pain—a remembrance always faint and unreal; but there was complete inability to revive the conditions that had engendered it.

How he had loved her and how he had suffered! especially during those first days, and even months, when he slept and waked dreaming of her; when his letters remained unanswered, and when existence was but a name for bitter endurance.

How long had it lasted? Could he tell? The end began when he could wake in the morning without the oppression, and free from the haunting pain. The end was that day, that hour or second, when he thought of her without emotion and without regret; as he thought of her now, with unstirred pulses. There was even with him now the touch of something keener than indifference—something engendered by revolt.

It was as if one loved, and dead and forgotten had returned to life; with the strange illusion that the rush of existence had halted while she lay in her grave; and with the still more singular delusion that love is eternal.

He did not hesitate as though confronted by a problem. He did not think of leaving the letter unnoticed. He did not think of telling her the truth. If he thought of these expedients, it was only to dismiss them.

He simply went to her. As he would have gone unflinchingly to meet the business obligation that he knew would leave him bankrupt.

"Two Summers and Two Souls." Written July 14, 1895. Published in *Vogue* (August 7, 1895).

# THE NIGHT CAME SLOWLY

I am losing my interest in human beings; in the significance of their lives and their actions. Some one has said it is better to study one man than ten books. I want neither books nor men; they make me suffer. Can one of them talk to me like the night—the Summer night? Like the stars or the caressing wind?

The night came slowly, softly, as I lay out there under the maple tree. It came creeping, creeping stealthily out of the valley, thinking I did not notice. And the outlines of trees and foliage nearby blended in one black mass and the night came stealing out from them, too, and from the east and west, until the only light was in the sky, filtering through the maple leaves and a star looking down through every cranny.

The night is solemn and it means mystery.

Human shapes flitted by like intangible things. Some stole

up like little mice to peep at me. I did not mind. My whole being was abandoned to the soothing and penetrating charm of the night.

The katydids began their slumber song: they are at it yet. How wise they are. They do not chatter like people. They tell me only: "sleep, sleep, sleep." The wind rippled the maple leaves like little warm love thrills.

Why do fools cumber the Earth! It was a man's voice that broke the necromancer's spell. A man came to-day with his "Bible Class." He is detestable with his red cheeks and bold eyes and coarse manner and speech. What does he know of Christ? Shall I ask a young fool who was born yesterday and will die tomorrow to tell me things of Christ? I would rather ask the stars: they have seen him.

"The Night Came Slowly." Written July 24, 1894. Published with "Juanita" under the title "A Scrap and a Sketch" in *Moods* (Philadelphia), July 1895.

# JUANITA

To all appearances and according to all accounts, Juanita is a character who does not reflect credit upon her family or her native town of Rock Springs. I first met her there three years ago in the little back room behind her father's store. She seemed very shy, and inclined to efface herself; a heroic feat to attempt, considering the narrow confines of the room; and a hopeless one, in view of her five-feet-ten, and more than two-hundred pounds of substantial flesh, which, on that occasion, and every subsequent one when I saw her, was clad in a soiled calico "Mother Hubbard."

Her face and particularly her mouth had a certain fresh and sensuous beauty, though I would rather not say "beauty" if I might say anything else.

I often saw Juanita that summer, simply because it was so difficult for the poor thing not to be seen. She usually sat in some obscure corner of their small garden, or behind an angle of the house, preparing vegetables for dinner or sorting her mother's flower-seed.

It was even at that day said, with some amusement, that Juanita was not so unattractive to men as her appearance might indicate; that she had more than one admirer, and great hopes of marrying well if not brilliantly.

Upon my return to the "Springs" this summer, in asking news of the various persons who had interested me three years ago, Juanita came naturally to my mind, and her name to my lips. There were many ready to tell me of Juanita's career since I had seen her.

The father had died and she and the mother had had ups and downs, but still continued to keep the store. Whatever else happened, however, Juanita had never ceased to attract admirers, young and old. They hung on her fence at all hours; they met her in the lanes; they penetrated to the store and back to the living-room. It was even talked about that a gentleman in a plaid suit had come all the way from the city by train for no other purpose than to call upon her. It is not astonishing, in face of these persistent attentions, that speculation grew rife in Rock Springs as to whom and what Juanita would marry in the end.

For a while she was said to be engaged to a wealthy south Missouri farmer, though no one could guess when or where she had met him. Then it was learned that the man of her choice was a Texas millionaire who possessed a hundred white horses, one of which spirited animals Juanita began to drive about that time.

But in the midst of speculation and counter speculation on the subject of Juanita and her lovers, there suddenly appeared upon the scene a one-legged man; a very poor and shabby, and decidedly one-legged man. He first became known to the public through Juanita's soliciting subscriptions towards buying the unhappy individual a cork-leg.

Her interest in the one-legged man continued to show itself in various ways, not always apparent to a curious public; as was proven one morning when Juanita became the mother of a baby, whose father, she announced, was her husband, the one-legged man. The story of a wandering preacher was told; a secret marriage in the state of Illinois; and a lost certificate.

However that may be, Juanita has turned her broad back upon the whole race of masculine bipeds, and lavishes the wealth of her undivided affections upon the one-legged man.

I caught a glimpse of the curious couple when I was in the village. Juanita had mounted her husband upon a dejected looking pony which she herself was apparently leading by the bridle, and they were moving up the lane towards the woods, whither, I am told, they often wander in this manner. The picture which they presented was a singular one; she with a man's big straw hat shading her inflamed moon-face, and the breeze bellying her soiled "Mother Hubbard" into monstrous proportions. He puny, helpless, but apparently content with his fate which had not even vouchsafed him the coveted cork-leg.

They go off thus to the woods together where they may love each other away from all prying eyes save those of the birds and the squirrels. But what do the squirrels care!

For my part I never expected Juanita to be more respectable than a squirrel; and I don't see how any one else could have expected it.

"Juanita." Written July 26, 1894. Published with "The Night Came Slowly" under the title "A Scrap and a Sketch" in *Moods* (Philadelphia), July 1895.

# THE UNEXPECTED

When Randall, for a brief absence, left his Dorothea, whom he was to marry after a time, the parting was bitter; the enforced separation seemed to them too cruel an ordeal to bear. The good-bye dragged with lingering kisses and sighs, and more kisses and more clinging till the last wrench came.

He was to return at the close of the month. Daily letters, impassioned and interminable, passed between them.

He did not return at the close of the month; he was delayed by illness. A heavy cold, accompanied by fever, contracted in some unaccountable way, held him to his bed. He hoped it would be over and that he would rejoin her in a week. But this was a stubborn cold, that seemed not to yield to familiar treatment; yet the physician was not discouraged, and promised to have him on his feet in a fortnight.

All this was torture to the impatient Dorothea; and if her

parents had permitted, she surely would have hastened to the bedside of her beloved.

For a long interval he could not write himself. One day he seemed better; another day a "fresh cold" seized him with relentless clutch; and so a second month went by, and Dorothea had reached the limit of her endurance.

Then a tremulous scrawl came from him, saying he would be obliged to pass a season at the south; but he would first revisit his home, if only for a day, to clasp his dearest one to his heart, to appease the hunger for her presence, the craving for her lips that had been devouring him through all the fever and pain of this detestable illness.

Dorothea had read his impassioned letters almost to tatters. She had sat daily gazing for hours upon his portrait, which showed him to be an almost perfect specimen of youthful health, strength and manly beauty.

She knew he would be altered in appearance—he had prepared her, and had even written that she would hardly know him. She expected to see him ill and wasted; she would not seem shocked; she would not let him see astonishment or pain in her face. She was in a quiver of anticipation, a sensuous fever of expectancy till he came.

She sat beside him on the sofa, for after the first delirious embrace he had been unable to hold himself upon his tottering feet, and had sunk exhausted in a corner of the sofa. He threw his head back upon the cushions and stayed, with closed eyes, panting; all the strength of his body had concentrated in the clasp—the grasp with which he clung to her hand.

She stared at him as one might look upon a curious apparition which inspired wonder and mistrust rather than fear. This was not the man who had gone away from her; the man she loved and had promised to marry. What hideous transformation had he undergone, or what devilish transformation was she undergoing in contemplating him? His skin was waxy and hectic, red upon the cheek-bones. His eyes were sunken; his features pinched and prominent; and his clothing hung loosely upon his wasted frame. The lips with which he had kissed her so hungrily, and with which he was kissing her now, were dry and parched, and his breath was feverish and tainted.

At the sight and the touch of him something within her seemed to be shuddering, shrinking, shriveling together, losing all semblance of what had been. She felt as if it was her heart; but it was only her love.

"This is the way my Uncle Archibald went—in a gallop—you know." He spoke with a certain derision and in little gasps, as if breath were failing him. "There's no danger of that for me, of course, once I get south; but the doctors won't answer for me if I stay here during the coming fall and winter."

Then he held her in his arms with what seemed to be a frenzy of passion; a keen and quickened desire beside which his former and healthful transports were tempered and lukewarm by comparison.

"We need not wait, Dorothea," he whispered. "We must not put it off. Let the marriage be at once, and you will come with me and be with me. Oh, God! I feel as if I would never let you go; as if I must hold you in my arms forever, night and day, and always!"

She attempted to withdraw from his embrace. She begged him not to think of it, and tried to convince him that it was impossible.

"I would only be a hindrance, Randall. You will come back well and strong; it will be time enough then," and to herself she was saying: "never, never, never!" There was a long silence, and he had closed his eyes again.

"For another reason, my Dorothea," and then he waited again, as one hesitates through shame or through fear, to speak.

"I am quite—almost sure I shall get well; but the strongest of us cannot count upon life. If the worst should come I want you to have all I possess; what fortune I have must be yours, and marriage will make my wish secure. Now I'm getting morbid." He ended with a laugh that died away in a cough which threatened to wrench the breath from his body, and which brought the attendant, who had waited without, quickly to his side.

Dorothea watched him from the window descend the steps, leaning upon the man's arm, and saw him enter his carriage and fall helpless and exhausted as he had sunk an hour before in the corner of her sofa.

She was glad there was no one present to compel her to speak. She stayed at the window as if dazed, looking fixedly at the spot where the carriage had stood. A clock on the mantel striking the hour finally roused her, and she realized that there would soon be people appearing whom she would be forced to face and speak to.

Fifteen minutes later Dorothea had changed her house gown, had mounted her "wheel," and was fleeing as if Death himself pursued her.

She sped along the familiar roadway, seemingly borne on by some force other than mechanical—some unwonted energy—a stubborn impulse that lighted her eyes, set her cheeks aflame, bent her supple body to one purpose—that was, swiftest flight.

How far, and how long did she go? She did not know; she did not care. The country about her grew unfamiliar. She was on a rough, unfrequented road, where the birds in the wayside bushes seemed unafraid. She could perceive no human habitation; an old fallow field, a stretch of wood, great trees bending thick-leaved branches, languidly, and flinging long, inviting shadows aslant the road; the weedy smell of summer; the drone of the insects; the sky and the clouds, and the quivering, lambent air. She was alone with nature; her pulses beating in unison with its sensuous throb, as she stopped and stretched herself upon the sward. Every muscle, nerve, fibre abandoned itself to the delicious sensation of rest that overtook and crept tingling through the whole length of her body.

She had never spoken a word after bidding him good-bye; but now she seemed disposed to make confidants of the tremulous leaves, or the crawling and hopping insects, or the big sky into which she was staring.

"Never!" she whispered, "not for all his thousands! Never, never! not for millions!"

"The Unexpected." Written July 18, 1895. Published in *Vogue* (September 18, 1895).

# HER LETTERS

## I

She had given orders that she wished to remain undisturbed and moreover had locked the doors of her room.

The house was very still. The rain was falling steadily from a leaden sky in which there was no gleam, no rift, no promise. A generous wood fire had been lighted in the ample fireplace and it brightened and illumined the luxurious apartment to its furthermost corner.

From some remote nook of her writing desk the woman took a thick bundle of letters, bound tightly together with strong, coarse twine, and placed it upon the table in the centre of the room.

For weeks she had been schooling herself for what she was about to do. There was a strong deliberation in the lines of her long, thin, sensitive face; her hands, too, were long and delicate and blue-veined.

With a pair of scissors she snapped the cord binding the letters together. Thus released the ones which were top-most slid down to the table and she, with a quick movement thrust her fingers among them, scattering and turning them over till they quite covered the broad surface of the table.

Before her were envelopes of various sizes and shapes, all of them addressed in the handwriting of one man and one woman. He had sent her letters all back to her one day when, sick with dread of possibilities, she had asked to have them returned. She had meant, then, to destroy them all, his and her own. That was four years ago, and she had been feeding upon them ever since; they had sustained her, she believed, and kept her spirit from perishing utterly.

But now the days had come when the premonition of danger could no longer remain unheeded. She knew that before many months were past she would have to part from her treasure, leaving it unguarded. She shrank from inflicting the pain, the anguish which the discovery of those letters would bring to others; to one, above all, who was near to her, and whose tenderness and years of devotion had made him, in a manner, dear to her.

She calmly selected a letter at random from the pile and cast it into the roaring fire. A second one followed almost as calmly, with the third her hand began to tremble; when, in a sudden paroxysm she cast a fourth, a fifth, and a sixth into the flames in breathless succession.

Then she stopped and began to pant—for she was far from strong, and she stayed staring into the fire with pained and savage eyes. Oh, what had she done! What had she not done! With feverish apprehension she began to search among the letters before her. Which of them had she so ruthlessly, so cruelly put out of her existence? Heaven grant, not the first, that very first one, written before they had learned, or dared to say to each other "I love you." No, no; there it was, safe enough. She laughed with pleasure, and held it to her lips. But what if that other most precious and most imprudent one were missing! in which every word of untempered passion had long ago eaten its way into her brain; and which stirred her still to-day, as it had done a hundred times before when she thought of it. She crushed it between her palms when she found it. She kissed it again and again. With her sharp white teeth she tore the far corner from the letter, where the name was written; she bit the torn scrap and tasted it between her lips and upon her tongue like some god-given morsel.

What unbounded thankfulness she felt at not having destroyed them all! How desolate and empty would have been her remaining days without them; with only her thoughts, illusive thoughts that she could not hold in her hands and press, as she did these, to her cheeks and her heart.

This man had changed the water in her veins to wine, whose taste had brought delirium to both of them. It was all one and past now, save for these letters that she held encircled in her arms. She stayed breathing softly and contentedly, with the hectic cheek resting upon them.

She was thinking, thinking of a way to keep them without possible ultimate injury to that other one whom they would stab more cruelly than keen knife blades.

At last she found the way. It was a way that frightened and bewildered her to think of at first, but she had reached it by deduction too sure to admit of doubt. She meant, of course, to destroy them herself before the end came. But how does the end come and when? Who may tell? She would guard against the possibility of accident by leaving them in charge of the very one who, above all, should be spared a knowledge of their contents.

She roused herself from the stupor of thought and gathered the scattered letters once more together, binding them again with the rough twine. She wrapped the compact bundle in a thick sheet of white polished paper. Then she wrote in ink upon the back of it, in large, firm characters:

"I leave this package to the care of my husband. With perfect faith in his loyalty and his love, I ask him to destroy it unopened."

It was not sealed; only a bit of string held the wrapper, which she could remove and replace at will whenever the humor came to her to pass an hour in some intoxicating dream of the days when she felt she had lived.

## II

If he had come upon that bundle of letters in the first flush of his poignant sorrow there would not have been an instant's hesitancy. To destroy it promptly and without question would have seemed a welcome expression of devotion—a way of reaching her, of crying out his love to her while the world was still filled with the illusion of her presence. But months had passed since that spring day when they had found her stretched upon the floor, clutching the key of her writing desk, which she appeared to have been attempting to reach when death overtook her.

The day was much like that day a year ago when the leaves were falling and rain pouring steadily from a leaden sky which held no gleam, no promise. He had happened accidentally upon the package in that remote nook of her desk. And just as she herself had done a year ago, he carried it to the table and laid it down there, standing, staring with puzzled eyes at the message which confronted him:

"I leave this package to the care of my husband. With perfect faith in his loyalty and his love, I ask him to destroy it unopened."

She had made no mistake; every line of his face—no longer young—spoke loyalty and honesty, and his eyes were as faithful as a dog's and as loving. He was a tall, powerful man, standing there in the firelight, with shoulders that stooped a little, and hair that was growing somewhat thin and gray, and a face that was distinguished, and must have been handsome when he smiled. But he was slow. "Destroy it unopened," he reread, half-aloud, "but why unopened?"

He took the package again in his hands, and turning it about and feeling it, discovered that it was composed of many letters tightly packed together.

So here were letters which she was asking him to destroy unopened. She had never seemed in her lifetime to have had a secret from him. He knew her to have been cold and passionless, but true, and watchful of his comfort and his happiness. Might he not be holding in his hands the secret of some other one, which had been confided to her and which she had promised to guard? But, no, she would have indicated the fact by some additional word or line. The secret was her own, something contained in these letters, and she wanted it to die with her.

If he could have thought of her as on some distant shadowy shore waiting for him throughout the years with outstretched hands to come and join her again, he would not have hesitated. With hopeful confidence he would have thought "in that blessed meeting-time, soul to soul, she will tell me all; till then I can wait and trust." But he could not think of her in any far-off paradise awaiting him. He felt that there was no smallest part of her anywhere in the universe, more than there had been before she was born into the world. But she had embodied herself with terrible significance in an intangible wish, uttered when life still coursed through her veins; knowing that it would reach him when the annihilation of death was between them, but uttered with all confidence in its power and potency. He was moved by the splendid daring of the act, which at the same time exalted him and lifted him above the head of common mortals.

What secret save one could a woman choose to have die with her? As quickly as the suggestion came to his mind, so swiftly did the man-instinct of possession stir in his blood. His fingers cramped about the package in his hands, and he sank into a chair beside the table. The agonizing suspicion that perhaps another had shared with him her thoughts, her affections, her life, deprived him for a swift instant of honor and reason. He thrust the end of his strong thumb beneath the string which, with a single turn would have yielded—"with perfect faith in your loyalty and your love." It was not the written characters addressing themselves to the eye; it was like a voice speaking to his soul. With a tremor of anguish he bowed his head down upon the letters.

A half-hour passed before he lifted his head. An unspeakable conflict had raged within him, but his loyalty and his love had conquered. His face was pale and deep-lined with suffering, but there was no more hesitancy to be seen there.

He did not for a moment think of casting the thick package into the flames to be licked by the fiery tongues, and charred and half-revealed to his eyes. That was not what she meant. He arose, and taking a heavy bronze paper-weight from the table, bound it securely to the package. He walked to the window and looked out into the street below. Darkness had come, and it was still raining. He could hear the rain dashing against the window-panes, and could see it falling through the dull yellow rim of light cast by the lighted street lamp.

He prepared himself to go out, and when quite ready to leave the house thrust the weighted package into the deep pocket of his top-coat.

He did not hurry along the street as most people were doing at that hour, but walked with a long, slow, deliberate step, not seeming to mind the penetrating chill and rain driving into his face despite the shelter of his umbrella.

His dwelling was not far removed from the business section of the city; and it was not a great while before he found himself at the entrance of the bridge that spanned the river—the deep, broad, swift, black river dividing two States. He walked on and out to the very center of the structure. The wind was blowing fiercely and keenly. The darkness where he stood was impenetrable. The thousands of lights in the city he had left seemed like all the stars of heaven massed together, sinking into some distant mysterious horizon, leaving him alone in a black, boundless universe.

He drew the package from his pocket and leaning as far as he could over the broad stone rail of the bridge, cast it from him into the river. It fell straight and swiftly from his hand. He could not follow its descent through the darkness, nor hear its dip into the water far below. It vanished silently; seemingly into some inky unfathomable space. He felt as if he were flinging it back to her in that unknown world whither she had gone.

## III

An hour or two later he sat at his table in the company of several men whom he had invited that day to dine with him.

A weight had settled upon his spirit, a conviction, a certitude that there could be but one secret which a woman would choose to have die with her. This one thought was possessing him. It occupied his brain, keeping it nimble and alert with suspicion. It clutched his heart, making every breath of existence a fresh moment of pain.

The men about him were no longer the friends of yesterday; in each one he discerned a possible enemy. He attended absently to their talk. He was remembering how she had conducted herself toward this one and that one; striving to recall conversations, subtleties of facial expression that might have meant what he did not suspect at the moment, shades of meaning in words that had seemed the ordinary interchange of social amenities.

He led the conversation to the subject of women, probing these men for their opinions and experiences. There was not one but claimed some infallible power to command the affections of any woman whom his fancy might select. He had heard the empty boast before from the same group and had always met it with good-humored contempt. But tonight every flagrant, inane utterance was charged with a new meaning, revealing possibilities that he had hitherto never taken into account.

He was glad when they were gone. He was eager to be alone, not from any desire or intention to sleep. He was impatient to regain her room, that room in which she had lived a large portion of her life, and where he had found those letters. There must surely be more of them somewhere, he thought; some forgotten scrap, some written thought or expression lying unguarded by an inviolable command.

At the hour when he usually retired for the night he sat himself down before her writing desk and began the search of drawers, slides, pigeonholes, nooks and corners. He did not leave a scrap of anything unread. Many of the letters which he found were old; some he had read before; others were new to him. But in none did he find a faintest evidence that his wife had not been the true and loyal woman he had always believed her to be. The night was nearly spent before the fruitless search ended. The brief, troubled sleep which he snatched before his hour for rising was freighted with feverish, grotesque dreams, through all of which he could hear and could see dimly the dark river rushing by, carrying away his heart, his ambitions, his life.

But it was not alone in letters that women betrayed their emotions, he thought. Often he had known them, especially when in love, to mark fugitive, sentimental passages in books of verse or prose, thus expressing and revealing their own hidden thought. Might she not have done the same?

Then began a second and far more exhausting and arduous quest than the first, turning, page by page, the volumes that crowded her room—books of fiction, poetry, philosophy. She had read them all; but nowhere, by the shadow of a sign, could he find that the author had echoed the secret of her existence—the secret which he had held in his hands and had cast into the river.

He began cautiously and gradually to question this one and that one, striving to learn by indirect ways what each had thought of her. Foremost he learned she had been unsympathetic because of her coldness of manner. One had admired her intellect; another her accomplishments; a third had thought her beautiful before disease claimed her, regretting, however, that her beauty had lacked warmth of color and expression. She was praised by some for gentleness and kindness, and by others for cleverness and tact. Oh, it was useless to try to discover anything from men! He might have known. It was women who would talk of what they knew.

They did talk, unreservedly. Most of them had loved her; those who had not had held her in respect and esteem.

## IV

And yet, and yet, "there is but one secret which a woman would choose to have die with her," was the thought which continued to haunt him and deprive him of rest. Days and nights of uncertainty began slowly to unnerve him and to torture him. An assurance of the worst that he dreaded would have offered him peace most welcome, even at the price of happiness.

It seemed no longer of any moment to him that men should come and go; and fall or rise in the world; and wed and die. It did not signify if money came to him by a turn of chance or eluded him. Empty and meaningless seemed to him all devices which the world offers for man's entertainment. The food and the drink set before him had lost their flavor. He did not longer know or care if the sun shone or the clouds lowered about him. A cruel hazard had struck him there where he was weakest, shattering his whole being, leaving him with but one wish in his soul, one gnawing desire, to know the mystery which he had held in his hands and had cast into the river.

One night when there were no stars shining he wandered, restless, upon the streets. He no longer sought to know from men and women what they dared not or could not tell him. Only the river knew. He went and stood again upon the bridge where he had stood many an hour since that night when the darkness then had closed around him and engulfed his manhood.

Only the river knew. It babbled, and he listened to it, and it told him nothing, but it promised all. He could hear it promising him with caressing voice, peace and sweet repose. He could hear the sweep, the song of the water inviting him.

A moment more and he had gone to seek her, and to join her and her secret thought in the immeasurable rest.

"Her Letters." Written November 29, 1894. Published in *Vogue* (April 11, 18, 1895).

# THE KISS

It was still quite light out of doors, but inside with the curtains drawn and the smouldering fire sending out a dim, uncertain glow, the room was full of deep shadows.

Brantain sat in one of these shadows; it had overtaken him and he did not mind. The obscurity lent him courage to keep his eyes fastened as ardently as he liked upon the girl who sat in the firelight.

She was very handsome, with a certain fine, rich coloring that belongs to the healthy brune type. She was quite composed, as she idly stroked the satiny coat of the cat that lay curled in her lap, and she occasionally sent a slow glance into the shadow where her companion sat. They were talking low, of indifferent things which plainly were not the things that occupied their thoughts. She knew that he loved her—a frank, blustering fellow without guile enough to conceal his feelings, and no desire to do so. For two weeks past he had sought her society eagerly and persistently. She was confidently waiting for him to declare himself and she meant to accept him. The rather insignificant and unattractive Brantain was enormously rich; and she liked and required the entourage which wealth could give her.

During one of the pauses between their talk of the last tea and the next reception the door opened and a young man entered whom Brantain knew quite well. The girl turned her face toward him. A stride or two brought him to her side, and bending over her chair—before she could suspect his intention, for she did not realize that he had not seen her visitor—he pressed an ardent, lingering kiss upon her lips.

Brantain slowly arose; so did the girl arise, but quickly, and the newcomer stood between them, a little amusement and some defiance struggling with the confusion in his face.

"I believe," stammered Brantain, "I see that I have stayed too long. I—I had no idea—that is, I must wish you good-bye." He was clutching his hat with both hands, and probably did not perceive that she was extending her hand to him, her presence of mind had not completely deserted her; but she could not have trusted herself to speak.

"Hang me if I saw him sitting there, Nattie! I know it's deuced awkward for you. But I hope you'll forgive me this once—this very first break. Why, what's the matter?"

"Don't touch me; don't come near me," she returned angrily. "What do you mean by entering the house without ringing?"

"I came in with your brother, as I often do," he answered coldly, in self-justification. "We came in the side way. He went upstairs and I came in here hoping to find you. The explanation is simple enough and ought to satisfy you that the misadventure was unavoidable. But do say that you forgive me, Nathalie," he entreated, softening.

"Forgive you! You don't know what you are talking about. Let me pass. It depends upon—a good deal whether I ever forgive you."

At that next reception which she and Brantain had been talking about she approached the young man with a delicious frankness of manner when she saw him there.

"Will you let me speak to you a moment or two, Mr. Brantain?" she asked with an engaging but perturbed smile. He seemed extremely unhappy; but when she took his arm and walked away with him, seeking a retired corner, a ray of hope mingled with the almost comical misery of his expression. She was apparently very outspoken.

"Perhaps I should not have sought this interview, Mr. Brantain; but—but, oh, I have been very uncomfortable, almost miserable since that little encounter the other afternoon. When I thought how you might have misinterpreted it, and believed things"—hope was plainly gaining the ascendancy over misery in Brantain's round, guileless face—"of course, I know it is nothing to you, but for my own sake I do want you to understand that Mr. Harvy is an intimate friend of long standing. Why, we have always been like cousins—like brother and sister, I may say. He is my brother's most intimate associate and often fancies that he is entitled to the same privileges as the family. Oh, I know it is absurd, uncalled for, to tell you this; undignified even," she was almost weeping, "but it makes so much difference to me what you think of—of me." Her voice had grown very low and agitated. The misery had all disappeared from Brantain's face.

"Then you do really care what I think, Miss Nathalie? May I call you Miss Nathalie?" They turned into a long, dim corridor that was lined on either side with tall, graceful plants. They walked slowly to the very end of it. When they turned to retrace their steps Brantain's face was radiant and hers was triumphant.

Harvy was among the guests at the wedding; and he sought her out in a rare moment when she stood alone.

"Your husband," he said, smiling, "has sent me over to kiss you."

A quick blush suffused her face and round polished throat. "I suppose it's natural for a man to feel and act generously on an occasion of this kind. He tells me he doesn't want his marriage to interrupt wholly that pleasant intimacy which has existed between you and me. I don't know what you've been telling him," with an insolent smile, "but he has sent me here to kiss you."

She felt like a chess player who, by the clever handling of his pieces, sees the game taking the course intended. Her eyes were bright and tender with a smile as they glanced up into his; and her lips looked hungry for the kiss which they invited.

"But, you know," he went on quietly, "I didn't tell him so, it would have seemed ungrateful, but I can tell you. I've stopped kissing women; it's dangerous."

Well, she had Brantain and his million left. A person can't have everything in this world; and it was a little unreasonable of her to expect it.

"The Kiss." Written September 19, 1894. Published in *Vogue* (January 17, 1895).

# SUZETTE

Ma'me Zidore thrust her head in at the window to tell Suzette that Michel Jardeau was dead.

"Ah, bon Dieu!" cried the girl, clasping her hands, "c' pauv' Michel!"

Ma'me Zidore had heard the news from one of Chartrand's "hands" who was passing with his wagon through the cut-off when she was gathering wood. Her old back was at that moment bent beneath the fagots. She spoke loud and noisily in shrill outbursts. With her unsteady, claw-like fingers she kept brushing aside the wisp of wiry gray hair that fell across her withered cheek.

She knew the story from beginning to end. Michel had boarded the Grand Ecore flat that very morning at daybreak. Jules Bat, the ferry man, had found him waiting on the bank to cross when he carried the doctor over to see Racell's sick child. He could not say whether Michel were drunk or not; he was gruff and ill-humored and seemed to be half asleep. Ma'me Zidore thought it highly probable that the young man had been carousing all night and was still under the influence of liquor when he lost his balance and fell into the water. A half dozen times Jules Bat had called out to him, warning him of his danger, for he persisted in standing at the open end of the boat. Then all in one miserable second over he went like a log. The water was high and turbid as a boiling caldron. Jules Bat saw no more of him than if he had been so many pounds of lead dropped into Red River.

A few people had assembled at their gates across the way, having gathered from snatches of the old woman's penetrating tones that something of interest had happened. She left Suzette standing at the window and crossed the road slant-wise, her whole gaunt frame revealing itself through her scanty, worn garments as the soft, swift breeze struck her old body.

"Michel Jardeau est mort!" she croaked, telling her news so suddenly that the women all cried out in dismay, and little Pavie Ombre, who was just reviving from a spell of sickness, uttered not a sound, but swayed to and fro and sank gently down on her knees in a white, dead faint.

Suzette retired into the room and approaching the tiny mirror that hung above the chest of drawers proceeded to finish her toilet in which task she had been interrupted by Ma'me Zidore's abrupt announcement of Michel Jardeau's death.

The girl every little while muttered under her breath:

"C' pauv' Michel." Yet her eyes were quite dry; they gleamed, but not with tears. Regret over the loss of "poor Michel" was in nowise distracting her attention from the careful arrangement of a bunch of carnations in the coils of her lustrous brown hair.

Yet she was thinking of him and wondering why she did not care.

A year ago—not so long as that—she had loved him desperately. It began that day at the barbecue when, seized with sudden infatuation, he stayed beside her the whole day long; turning her head with his tones, his glances, and soft touches. Before that day he had seemed to care for little Pavie Ombre who had come out of her faint and was now wailing and sobbing across the way, indifferent to those who might hear her in passing along the road. But after that day he cared no longer for Pavie Ombre or any woman on earth besides Suzette. What a weariness that love had finally become to her, only herself knew.

Why did he persist? why could he not have understood? His attentions had fretted her beyond measure; it was torture to feel him there every Sunday at Mass with his eyes fastened upon her during the entire service. It was not her fault that he had grown desperate—that he was dead.

She turned her head this way and that way before the small glass, noting the effect of the carnations in her hair. She gave light touches to the trimmings about her neck and waist, and adjusted the puffed sleeves of her white gown. She moved about the small room with a certain suppressed agitation, returning often to the mirror, and sometimes straying to the window.

Suzette was standing there when a sound arrested her attention—the distant tramp of an advancing herd of cattle. It was what she had been waiting for; what she had been listening for. Yet she trembled through her whole supple frame when she heard it, and the color began to mount into her cheeks. She stayed there at the window looking like a painted picture in its frame.

The house was small and low and stood a little back, with no enclosing fence about the grass plot that reached from the window quite to the edge of the road.

All was still, save for the tramp of the advancing herd. There was no dust, for it had rained during the morning; and Suzette could see them now, approaching with slow, swinging motion and tossing of long horns. Mothers had run out, gathering and snatching their little ones from the road. Baptiste, one of the drivers, shouted hoarsely, cracking his long whip, while a couple of dogs tore madly around, snapping and barking.

The other driver, a straight-backed young fellow, sat his horse with familiar ease and carelessness. He wore a white flannel shirt, coarse trousers and leggings and a broad-brimmed gray felt. From the moment his figure appeared in sight, Suzette did not remove her eyes from him. The glow in her cheeks was resplendent now.

She was feeling in anticipation the penetration of his glance, the warmth of his smile when he should see her. He would ride up to the window, no doubt, to say good-bye, and she would give him the carnations as a remembrance to keep till he came back.

But what did he mean? She turned a little chill with apprehension. Why, at that precious moment should he bother about the unruly beast that seemed bent upon making trouble? And there was that idiot, that pig of a Baptiste pulling up on the other side of him—talking to him, holding his attention. *Mère de Dieu!* how she hated and could have killed the fool!

With a single impulse there was a sudden quickened movement of the herd—a dash forward. Then they went! with lowered, tossing heads, rounding the bend that sloped down to the ford.

He had passed! He had not looked at her! He had not thought of her! He would be gone three weeks—three eternities! and every hour freighted with the one bitter remembrance of his indifference!

Suzette turned from the window—her face gray and pinched, with all the warmth and color gone out of it. She flung herself upon the bed and there she cried and moaned with wrenching sobs between.

The carnations drooped from their fastening and lay like a bloodstain upon her white neck.

"Suzette." Written February 1897. Published in *Vogue* (October 21, 1897).

# THE FALLING IN LOVE OF FEDORA (FEDORA)

Fedora had determined upon driving over to the station herself for Miss Malthers.

Though one or two of them looked disappointed—notably her brother—no one opposed her. She said the brute was restive, and shouldn't be trusted to the handling of the young people.

To be sure Fedora was old enough, from the standpoint of her sister Camilla and the rest of them. Yet no one would ever have thought of it but for her own persistent affectation and idiotic assumption of superior years and wisdom. She was thirty.

Fedora had too early in life formed an ideal and treasured it. By this ideal she had measured such male beings as had hitherto challenged her attention, and needless to say she had found them wanting. The young people—her brothers' and sisters' guests, who were constantly coming and going that summer—occupied her to a great extent, but failed to interest her. She concerned herself with their comforts—in the absence of her mother—looked after their health and well-being; contrived for their amusements, in which she never joined. And, as Fedora was tall and slim, and carried her head loftily, and wore eye-glasses and a severe expression, some of them—the silliest—felt as if she were a hundred years old. Young Malthers thought she was about forty.

One day when he stopped before her out in the gravel walk to ask her some question pertaining to the afternoon's sport, Fedora, who was tall, had to look up into his face to answer him. She had known him eight years, since he was a lad of fifteen, and to her he had never been other than the lad of fifteen.

But that afternoon, looking up into his face, the sudden realization came home to her that he was a man—in voice, in attitude, in bearing, in every sense—a man.

In an absorbing glance, and with unaccountable intention, she gathered in every detail of his countenance as though it were a strange, new thing to her, presenting itself to her vision for the first time. The eyes were blue, earnest, and at the moment a little troubled over some trivial affair that he was relating to her. The face was brown from the sun, smooth, with no suggestion of ruddiness, except in the lips, that were strong, firm and clean. She kept thinking of his face, and every trick of it after he passed on.

From that moment he began to exist for her. She looked at him when he was near by, she listened for his voice, and took notice and account of what he said. She sought him out; she selected him when occasion permitted. She wanted him by her, though his nearness troubled her. There was uneasiness, restlessness, expectation when he was not there within sight or sound. There was redoubled uneasiness when he was by—there was inward revolt, astonishment, rapture, self-contumely; a swift, fierce encounter betwixt thought and feeling.

Fedora could hardly explain to her own satisfaction why she wanted to go herself to the station for young Malthers's sister. She felt a desire to see the girl, to be near her; as unaccountable, when she tried to analyze it, as the impulse which drove her, and to which she often yielded, to touch his hat, hanging with others upon the hall pegs, when she passed it by. Once a coat which he had discarded hung there too. She handled it under pretense of putting it in order. There was no one near, and, obeying a sudden impulse, she buried her face for an instant in the rough folds of the coat.

Fedora reached the station a little before train time. It was in a pretty nook, green and fragrant, set down at the foot of a wooded hill. Off in a clearing there was a field of yellow grain, upon which the sinking sunlight fell in slanting, broken beams. Far down the track there were some men at work, and the even ring of their hammers was the only sound that broke upon the stillness. Fedora loved it all—sky and woods and sunlight; sounds and smells. But her bearing—elegant, composed, reserved—betrayed nothing emotional as she tramped the narrow platform, whip in hand, and occasionally offered a condescending word to the mail man or the sleepy agent.

Malthers's sister was the only soul to disembark from the train. Fedora had never seen her before; but if there had been a hundred, she would have known the girl. She was a small thing; but aside from that, there was the coloring; there were the blue, earnest eyes; there, above all, was the firm, full curve of the lips; the same setting of the white, even teeth. There was the subtle play of feature, the elusive trick of expression, which she had thought peculiar and individual in the one, presenting themselves as family traits.

The suggestive resemblance of the girl to her brother was vivid, poignant even to Fedora, realizing, as she did with a pang, that familiarity and custom would soon blur the image.

Miss Malthers was a quiet, reserved creature, with little to say. She had been to college with Camilla, and spoke somewhat of their friendship and former intimacy. She sat lower in the cart than Fedora, who drove, handling whip and rein with accomplished skill.

"You know, dear child," said Fedora, in her usual elderly fashion, "I want you to feel completely at home with us." They were driving through a long, quiet, leafy road, into which the twilight was just beginning to creep. "Come to me freely and without reserve—with all your wants; with any complaints. I feel that I shall be quite fond of you."

She had gathered the reins into one hand, and with the other free arm she encircled Miss Malthers's shoulders.

When the girl looked up into her face, with murmured thanks, Fedora bent down and pressed a long, penetrating kiss upon her mouth.

Malthers's sister appeared astonished, and not too well pleased. Fedora, with seemingly unruffled composure, gathered the reins, and for the rest of the way stared steadily ahead of her between the horses' ears.

"The Falling in Love of Fedora." Written November 19, 1895. Published in *St. Louis Criterion* (February 20, 1897) under the pen name "La Tour." Later called "Fedora."

# THE RECOVERY

She was a woman of thirty-five, possessing something of youthfulness. It was not the bloom, the softness, nor delicacy of coloring which had once been hers; those were all gone. It lurked rather in the expression of her sensitive face, which was at once appealing, pathetic, confiding.

For fifteen years she had lived in darkness with closed lids. By one of those seeming miracles of science, and by slow and gradual stages, the light had been restored to her. Now, for the first time in many years, she opened her eyes upon the full, mellow brightness of a June day.

She was alone. She had asked to be alone at the very first. Glad almost to ecstasy, she was yet afraid. She wanted first to see the light from her open window; to look at the dumb inanimate objects around her before gazing into the dear familiar faces that were stamped with sharp and vivid impress upon her mind.

And how beautiful was the world from her open window!

"Oh, my God!" she whispered, overcome. Her prayer could get no further. There were no words to utter her rapture and thanksgiving at beholding the blue unfathomable June sky; the rolling meadows, russet and green, reaching deep into the purple distance. Close beside her window the maple leaves rippled in the sun; flowers, rich and warm in color, blossomed beneath, and radiant-winged butterflies hovered sensuous in mid-air.

"The world has not changed," she murmured; "it has only grown more beautiful. Oh, I had forgotten how beautiful!"

Within her room were all the dear, dumb companions comforting her. How well she remembered them all! Her mahogany table, bright and polished, just as it had stood fifteen years ago, with a crystal vase of roses and a few books ranged upon it. The sight of chairs, beds, pictures gave her keen joy. The carpet and draperies, even—with their designs as much like the old ones as could be—seemed to her the same.

She touched with caressing fingers the French clock upon the mantel with its pompous little bronze figure of a last-century gentleman posing in buckles and frills beside the dial. She greeted him as an old friend, and delicately wiped his little bronze face with her soft handkerchief. As a child she had thought him an imposing figure. At a later and over-discriminating age she had patronized him as a poor bit of art. Now, nothing could have induced her to part with the old French clock and its little bronze bonhomme.

The mirror was over there in the corner. She had not forgotten it; oh, no, she had not forgotten, only she grew tremulous at the thought of it standing there. She held back, as a young girl who is going to confession is ashamed and afraid, and invites delay. But she had not forgotten.

"This is folly," she uttered suddenly, passing the handkerchief nervously over her face. With quick resolution she crossed the room and faced her reflected image in the glass.

"Mother!" she cried, involuntarily, turning swiftly; but she was still alone. It had happened like a flash—an unreasoning impulse that knew not control or direction. She at once recovered herself and drew a deep breath. Again she wiped her forehead, that was a little clammy. She clutched the back of a low chair with her shaking hands and looked once more into the mirror. The veins in her wrists swelled like cords and throbbed.

You or I or anyone looking upon that same picture in the glass would have seen a rather well-preserved, stately blonde woman of thirty-five or more. Only God knows what she saw. It was something that held her with terrible fascination.

The eyes, above all, seemed to speak to her. Afflicted as they had been, they alone belonged to that old, other self that had somewhere vanished. She questioned, she challenged them. And while she looked down into their depths she drew into her soul all the crushing weight of the accumulated wisdom of years.

"They lied; they all lied to me," she said, half aloud, never taking her eyes from those others. "Mother, sisters, Robert—all, all of them lied."

When the eyes in the glass had nothing more to tell her, she turned away from them. The pathos of her face had vanished; there was no longer the appeal that had been there a while ago; neither was there confidence.

The following day she walked abroad leaning upon the arm of the man whose untiring devotion to her had persisted for years. She would not fulfill her promise to marry him when blindness had overtaken her. He had endured the years of probation, wanting no other woman for his wife; living at her side when he could, and bringing himself close to her inner life by a warm, quick, watchful sympathy born of much love.

He was older than she—a man of splendid physique. The slim stripling of fifteen years ago was hardly the promise of this man of forty. His face had settled into a certain ruggedness accentuated by a few strong lines, and white hairs were beginning to show among the black ones on the temples.

They walked across the level stretch of lawn toward a sheltered garden seat no great distance away. She had spoken little since that moment of revelation before her mirror. Nothing had startled her after that. She was prepared for the changes which the years had wrought in all of them—mother, sisters, friends.

She seemed to be silently absorbing things, and would have lingered in ecstasy before a flower, or with her gaze penetrating the dense foliage beyond. Her senses had long been sharpened to the sounds and odors of the good, green world, and now her restored vision completed a sensuous impression such as she had never dreamed could be borne in upon a human consciousness.

He led her away to the bench. He fancied that seated he could better hold her attention to what was in his mind to say to her.

He took her hand in his. She was used to this and did not draw it away, but let it lie there.

"Do you remember the old plans, Jane?" he began, almost at once, "all that we were to have done, to have seen, all that we were going to live together? How we had chosen to start away in the early spring time upon our travels—you and I—and only come back with the frosts of winter. You have not forgotten, dearest?" He bent his face down over her hand and kissed it. "The spring is over; but we have the summer with us, and God willing, the autumn and winter left to us. Tell me, Jane—tell me—speak to me!" he entreated.

She looked into his face and then away, and back again, uncertainly.

"I—oh, Robert," she said, gropingly, "wait—I—the sight of things confuses me," and with a faint smile, "I am not used; I must go back into the dark to think."

He still held her hand, but she turned half away from him and buried her face in her arm that she leaned upon the back of the garden seat.

What could she hope to gather from the darkness that the light had not given her! She might hope, and she might wait and she might pray; but hope and prayer and waiting would avail her nothing.

The blessed light had given her back the world, life, love; but it had robbed her of her illusions; it had stolen away her youth.

He drew close to her, pressing his face near hers for his answer; and all that he heard was a little low sob.

"The Recovery." Written February 1896. Published in *Vogue* (May 21, 1896), 354–355.

# THE BLIND MAN

A man carrying a small red box in one hand walked slowly down the street. His old straw hat and faded garments looked as if the rain had often beaten upon them, and the sun had as many times dried them upon his person. He was not old, but he seemed feeble; and he walked in the sun, along the blistering asphalt pavement. On the opposite side of the street there were trees that threw a thick and pleasant shade; people were all walking on that side. But the man did not know, for he was blind, and moreover he was stupid.

In the red box were lead pencils, which he was endeavoring to sell. He carried no stick, but guided himself by trailing his foot along the stone copings or his hand along the iron railings. When he came to the steps of a house he would mount them. Sometimes, after reaching the door with great difficulty, he could not find the electric button, whereupon he would patiently descend and go his way. Some of the iron gates were locked—their owners being away for the summer—and he would consume much time in striving to open them, which made little difference, as he had all the time there was at his disposal.

At times he succeeded in finding the electric button; but the man or maid who answered the bell needed no pencil, nor could they be induced to disturb the mistress of the house about so small a thing.

The man had been out long and had walked very far, but had sold nothing. That morning some one who had finally grown tired of having him hanging around had equipped him with this box of pencils, and sent him out to make his living. Hunger, with sharp fangs, was gnawing at his stomach and a consuming thirst parched his mouth and tortured him. The sun was broiling. He wore too much clothing—a vest and coat over his shirt. He might have removed these and carried them on his arm or thrown them away; but he did not think of it. A kind-hearted woman who saw him from an upper window felt sorry for him, and wished that he would cross over into the shade.

The man drifted into a side street, where there was a group of noisy, excited children at play. The color of the box which he carried attracted them and they wanted to know what was in it. One of them attempted to take it away from him. With the instinct to protect his own and his only means of sustenance, he resisted, shouted at the children and called them names. A policeman coming around the corner and seeing that he was the center of a disturbance, jerked him violently around by the collar; but upon perceiving that he was blind, considerately refrained from clubbing him and sent him on his way. He walked on in the sun.

During his aimless rambling he turned into a street where

there were monster electric cars thundering up and down, clanging wild bells and literally shaking the ground beneath his feet with their terrific impetus. He started to cross the street.

Then something happened—something horrible happened that made the women faint and the strongest men who saw it grow sick and dizzy. The motorman's lips were as gray as his face, and that was ashen gray; and he shook and staggered from the superhuman effort he had put forth to stop his car.

Where could the crowds have come from so suddenly, as if by magic? Boys on the run, men and women tearing up on their wheels to see the sickening sight; doctors dashing up in buggies as if directed by Providence.

And the horror grew when the multitude recognized in the dead and mangled figure one of the wealthiest, most useful and most influential men of the town—a man noted for his prudence and foresight. How could such a terrible fate have overtaken him? He was hastening from his business house—for he was late—to join his family, who were to start in an hour or two for their summer home on the Atlantic coast. In his hurry he did not perceive the other car coming from the opposite direction, and the common, harrowing thing was repeated.

The blind man did not know what the commotion was all about. He had crossed the street, and there he was, stumbling on in the sun, trailing his foot along the coping.

"The Blind Man." Written July, 1896. Published in *Vogue* (May 13, 1897).

# AN EASTER DAY CONVERSION (A MORNING WALK)

Archibald had been up many hours. He had breakfasted, and now he was taking a morning stroll along the village street, which was little other than a high ledge cut into the mountainside.

He was forty or thereabout, but did not resent being thought older, and never corrected the miscalculations of acquaintances when they added a half-score years to his age. He was tall, with broad shoulders, a straight back, and legs that took long, energetic strides. His hair was light and rather thin; his face strong and rugged from exposure, and his eyes narrow and observant. He beat about with his stick as he walked, turning over pebbles and small stones, and sometimes uprooting a weed or flower that grew in his path.

The village sprawled along the gradual slope of a mountainside. The few streets rising one above the other were irregular in their tortuous effort to cuddle up to the houses that were built haphazard and wide apart. Flights of wooden steps, black and weather-stained, connected the streets with each other. Fruit trees were in bloom, making a pink and white blur against the blue sky and the gray, rocky slopes. Birds were piping in the hedges. It had rained, but the sun was shining now and riotous odors were abroad; they met him with every velvety gust that softly beat into his face. Now and again he straightened his shoulders and shook his head with an impatient movement, as might some proud animal which rebels against an unaccustomed burden.

The spring was nothing new to him, nor were its sounds, its perfumes, its colors; nor was its tender and caressing breath; but, for some unaccountable reason, these were reaching him today through unfamiliar channels.

Archibald had started out for a walk, not because the day was beautiful and alluring but for the healthful exercise, and for the purpose of gathering into his lungs the amount of pure oxygen needed to keep his body in good working condition. For he leaned decidedly toward practical science; of sentiment he knew little, except what he gathered from a class of speculative philosophers. He liked to read musty books about musty peoples long since gathered to the earth and the elements. He liked to observe insect life at close range, and when he gathered flowers it was usually to dismember their delicate, sweet bodies for the purpose of practical and profitable investigation.

But, strangely enough, he saw only the color of the blossoms this morning, and noted their perfumes. The butterflies floated unmolested within his reach, and the jumping grasshoppers were not afraid. The spring day was saying "good morning" to him in a new, delicious way, while the blood in his veins beat a response.

A little ahead of him Archibald suddenly observed a huge

bunch of white lilies ascending apparently from the sepulchral depths of the earth. In fact they were ascending one of the steep flights of wooden steps which led up from the street below. A young girl's face could be seen between the long stems and the blossoms. In another moment she stood on the edge of the road, panting a little. She was pretty, as healthful girls of twenty usually are. She was unusually pretty at that moment; her face, peeping over the lilies, was like another flower that had gathered its hues from the roseate dawn and the glimmer of the dew.

"Good morning, Mr. Archibald," she called in her sweet, high, village voice.

"Good morning, Jane; good morning," he responded with unusual cordiality.

"Oh! it isn't Jane," she laughed, "it's Lucy. L-U-C-Y Lucy. Last week you persistently thought I was my sister Amanda. This morning I am my cousin Jane. Tomorrow I suppose it will be 'good morning, Mrs. Brockett'; or 'Howdy, Granny Ball!' "

A more delicately attuned ear than Archibald's might have detected a lurking note of vexation in the girl's saucy speech. He flushed with annoyance at his own awkwardness. Yesterday he would have smiled with condescending inattention, and probably called her "Amelia" at their next meeting.

"Yes," she was thinking, as they walked together down the road, "if I were a stone or a weed or some nasty old beetle or other, he would know my name well enough." She was one of a group of girls whom he had seen grow up in almost daily association with his own nieces and nephews at home. It was not to be expected that he could disassociate them. He regretted that there had been made no arbitrary classification of the family of "Girls," whereby a man of studious instincts and mental preoccupation might be able to identify the individual at sight, and even name it at a moment's notice. However, he felt quite sure that he would not soon forget that it was Lucy who carried the lilies and bade him good morning, like a second vision of spring.

"Let me carry your flowers," he offered; not through any tardy spirit of gallantry; solely because he knew better than she how to handle a bunch of blossoms, and it pained him to see the big wax-like petals bruised and jostled. The odor of the flowers was heavy and penetrating, like the fumes of a subtle intoxicant that reached Archibald's brain, and wrought and wove fantastic thoughts and visions there. He looked down into the girl's face, and her soft, curved lips made him think of peaches that he had bitten; of grapes that he had tasted; of a cup's rim from which he had sometimes sipped wine.

They walked down the grassy slope, the girl chatting the while, and Archibald saying little. Lucy was on her way to church. It was Easter morning, and the bells had been calling and clamoring to them as they went along. At the vestibule door she turned and delivered him of his burden of flowers. But Archibald did not leave there, as she expected he would. He followed her into the church; he did not know why, and for once he did not care to investigate his motives. When she had disposed of the lilies, turning them over to a sanctuary boy, she came and seated herself with the congregation, and Archibald, who had stood waiting, placed himself beside her. He assumed no reverential attitude, nor did he bow his head with any pretense of devotion. His presence caused much wonder, and glances and whispers of speculation were exchanged. Archibald did not notice, and would not have minded them if he had noticed.

The day was warm, and some of the stained glass windows were open. The sunlight came in, and the shadows of quivering leaves played upon the casement through which he gazed. A bird was singing among the branches.

During the prayers he was inattentive, and to the singing he lent no ear. But when the minister turned to address the assembly, Archibald wondered what he was going to say. The man stayed a long moment with his slow, earnest glance sweeping the congregation, then he uttered solemnly and impressively: "I am the Resurrection and the Life."

Another long moment of silence followed; and, lifting his head, he reiterated in louder, clearer tones than before, "I am the Resurrection and the Life."

This was his text. It fell upon ears that had heard it before. It crept into the consciousness of Archibald, sitting there. As he gathered it into his soul a vision of life came with it; the poet's vision, of life that is within and the life that is without, pulsing in unison, breathing the harmony of an undivided existence.

He listened to no further words of the minister. He entered into himself and he preached unto himself a sermon in his own heart, as he gazed from the window through which the song came and where the leafy shadows quivered.

"An Easter Day Conversion." Written April 1897, with the title "A Morning Walk." Published in *St. Louis Criterion* (April 17, 1897) under the title "An Easter Day Conversion."

# LILACS

Mme. Adrienne Farival never announced her coming; but the good nuns knew very well when to look for her. When the scent of the lilac blossoms began to permeate the air, Sister Agathe would turn many times during the day to the window; upon her face the happy, beatific expression with which pure and simple souls watch for the coming of those they love.

But it was not Sister Agathe; it was Sister Marceline who first espied her crossing the beautiful lawn that sloped up to the convent. Her arms were filled with great bunches of lilacs which she had gathered along her path. She was clad all in brown; like one of the birds that come with the spring, the nuns used to say. Her figure was rounded and graceful, and she walked with a happy, buoyant step. The cabriolet which had conveyed her to the convent moved slowly up the gravel drive that led to the imposing entrance. Beside the driver was her modest little black trunk, with her name and address printed in white letters upon it: "Mme. A. Farival, Paris." It was the crunching of the gravel which had attracted Sister Marceline's attention. And then the commotion began.

White-capped heads appeared suddenly at the windows; she waved her parasol and her bunch of lilacs at them. Sister Marceline and Sister Marie Anne appeared, fluttered and expectant at the doorway. But Sister Agathe, more daring and impulsive than all, descended the steps and flew across the grass to meet her. What embraces, in which the lilacs were crushed between them! What ardent kisses! What pink flushes of happiness mounting the cheeks of the two women!

Once within the convent Adrienne's soft brown eyes moistened with tenderness as they dwelt caressingly upon the familiar objects about her, and noted the most trifling details. The white, bare boards of the floor had lost nothing of their luster. The stiff, wooden chairs, standing in rows against the walls of hall and parlor, seemed to have taken on an extra polish since she had seen them, last lilac time. And there was a new picture of the Sacré-Coeur hanging over the hall table. What had they done with Ste. Catherine de Sienne, who had occupied that position of honor for so many years? In the chapel—it was no use trying to deceive her—she saw at a glance that St. Joseph's mantle had been embellished with a new coat of blue, and the aureole about his head freshly gilded. And the Blessed Virgin there neglected! Still wearing her garb of last spring, which looked almost dingy by contrast. It was not just—such partiality! The Holy Mother had reason to be jealous and to complain.

But Adrienne did not delay to pay her respects to the Mother Superior, whose dignity would not permit her to so much as step outside the door of her private apartments to welcome this old pupil. Indeed, she was dignity in person; large, uncompromising, unbending. She kissed Adrienne without warmth, and discussed conventional themes learnedly and prosaically during the quarter of an hour which the young woman remained in her company.

It was then that Adrienne's latest gift was brought in for inspection. For Adrienne always brought a handsome present for the chapel in her little black trunk. Last year it was a necklace of gems for the Blessed Virgin, which the Good Mother was only permitted to wear on extra occasions, such as great feast days of obligation. The year before it had been a precious crucifix—an ivory figure of Christ suspended from an ebony cross, whose extremities were tipped with wrought silver. This time it was a linen embroidered altar cloth of such rare and delicate workmanship that the Mother Superior, who knew the value of such things, chided Adrienne for the extravagance.

"But, dear Mother, you know it is the greatest pleasure I have in life—to be with you all once a year, and to bring some such trifling token of my regard."

The Mother Superior dismissed her with the rejoinder: "Make yourself at home, my child. Sister Thérèse will see to your wants. You will occupy Sister Marceline's bed in the end room, over the chapel. You will share the room with Sister Agathe."

There was always one of the nuns detailed to keep Adrienne company during her fortnight's stay at the convent. This had become almost a fixed regulation. It was only during the hours of recreation that she found herself with them all together. Those were hours of much harmless merry-making under the trees or in the nuns' refectory.

This time it was Sister Agathe who waited for her outside of the Mother Superior's door. She was taller and slenderer than Adrienne, and perhaps ten years older. Her fair blond face flushed and paled with every passing emotion that visited her soul. The two women linked arms and went together out into the open air.

There was so much which Sister Agathe felt that Adrienne must see. To begin with, the enlarged poultry yard, with its dozens upon dozens of new inmates. It took now all the time of one of the lay sisters to attend to them. There had been no change made in the vegetable garden, but—yes there had; Adrienne's quick eye at once detected it. Last year old Philippe had planted his cabbages in a large square to the right. This year they were set out in an oblong bed to the left. How it made Sister Agathe laugh to think Adrienne should have noticed such a trifle! And old Philippe, who was nailing a broken trellis not far off, was called forward to be told about it.

He never failed to tell Adrienne how well she looked, and how she was growing younger each year. And it was his delight to recall certain of her youthful and mischievous escapades. Never would he forget that day she disappeared; and the whole convent in a hubbub about it! And how at last it was he who discovered her perched among the tallest branches of the highest tree on the grounds, where she had climbed to see if she could get a glimpse of Paris! And her punishment afterwards!—half of the Gospel of Palm Sunday to learn by heart!

"We may laugh over it, my good Philippe, but we must remember that Madame is older and wiser now."

"I know well, Sister Agathe, that one ceases to commit follies after the first days of youth." And Adrienne seemed greatly impressed by the wisdom of Sister Agathe and old Philippe, the convent gardener.

A little later when they sat upon a rustic bench which overlooked the smiling landscape about them, Adrienne was saying to Sister Agathe, who held her hand and stroked it fondly:

"Do you remember my first visit, four years ago, Sister Agathe? and what a surprise it was to you all!"

"As if I could forget it, dear child!"

"And I! Always shall I remember that morning as I walked along the boulevard with a heaviness of heart—oh, a heaviness which I hate to recall. Suddenly there was wafted to me the sweet odor of lilac blossoms. A young girl had passed me by, carrying a great bunch of them. Did you ever know, Sister Agathe, that there is nothing which so keenly revives a memory as a perfume—an odor?"

"I believe you are right, Adrienne. For now that you speak of it, I can feel how the odor of fresh bread—when Sister Jeanne bakes—always makes me think of the great kitchen of ma tante de Sierge, and crippled Julie, who sat always knitting at the sunny window. And I never smell the sweet scented honeysuckle without living again through the blessed day of my first communion."

"Well, that is how it was with me, Sister Agathe, when the scent of the lilacs at once changed the whole current of my thoughts and my despondency. The boulevard, its noises, its passing throng, vanished from before my senses as completely as if they had been spirited away. I was standing here with my feet sunk in the green sward as they are now. I could see the sunlight glancing from that old white stone wall, could hear the notes of birds, just as we hear them now, and the humming of insects in the air. And through all I could see and could smell the lilac blossoms, nodding invitingly to me from their thick-leaved branches. It seems to me they are richer than ever this year, Sister Agathe. And do you know, I became like an *enragée*; nothing could have kept me back. I do not remember now where I was going; but I turned and retraced my steps homeward in a perfect fever of agitation: 'Sophie! my little trunk—quick—the black one! A mere handful of clothes! I am going away. Don't ask me any questions. I shall be back in a fortnight.' And every year since then it is the same. At the very first whiff of a lilac blossom, I am gone! There is no holding me back."

"And how I wait for you, and watch those lilac bushes, Adrienne! If you should once fail to come, it would be like the spring coming without the sunshine or the song of birds.

"But do you know, dear child, I have sometimes feared that in moments of despondency such as you have just described, I fear that you do not turn as you might to our Blessed Mother in heaven, who is ever ready to comfort and solace an afflicted heart with the precious balm of her sympathy and love."

"Perhaps I do not, dear Sister Agathe. But you cannot picture the annoyances which I am constantly submitted to. That Sophie alone, with her detestable ways! I assure you she of herself is enough to drive me to St. Lazare."

"Indeed, I do understand that the trials of one living in the world must be very great, Adrienne; particularly for you, my poor child, who have to bear them alone, since Almighty God was pleased to call to himself your dear husband. But on the other hand, to live one's life along the lines which our dear Lord traces for each one of us, must bring with it resignation and even a certain comfort. You have your household duties, Adrienne, and your music, to which, you say, you continue to devote yourself. And then, there are always good works—the poor—who are always with us—to be relieved; the afflicted to be comforted."

"But, Sister Agathe! Will you listen! Is it not La Rose that I hear moving down there at the edge of the pasture? I fancy she is reproaching me with being an ingrate, not to have pressed a kiss yet on that white forehead of hers. Come, let us go."

The two women arose and walked again, hand in hand this

time, over the tufted grass down the gentle decline where it sloped toward the broad, flat meadow, and the limpid stream that flowed cool and fresh from the woods. Sister Agathe walked with her composed, nunlike tread; Adrienne with a balancing motion, a bounding step, as though the earth responded to her light footfall with some subtle impulse all its own.

They lingered long upon the foot-bridge that spanned the narrow stream which divided the convent grounds from the meadow beyond. It was to Adrienne indescribably sweet to rest there in soft, low converse with this gentle-faced nun, watching the approach of evening. The gurgle of the running water beneath them; the lowing of cattle approaching in the distance, were the only sounds that broke upon the stillness, until the clear tones of the angelus bell pealed out from the convent tower. At the sound both women instinctively sank to their knees, signing themselves with the sign of the cross. And Sister Agathe repeated the customary invocation, Adrienne responding in musical tones:

"The Angel of the Lord declared unto Mary,
And she conceived by the Holy Ghost—"

and so forth, to the end of the brief prayer, after which they arose and retraced their steps toward the convent.

It was with subtle and naïve pleasure that Adrienne prepared herself that night for bed. The room which she shared with Sister Agathe was immaculately white. The walls were a dead white, relieved only by one florid print depicting Jacob's dream at the foot of the ladder, upon which angels mounted and descended. The bare floors, a soft yellow-white, with two little patches of gray carpet beside each spotless bed. At the head of the white-draped beds were two *bénitiers* containing holy water absorbed in sponges.

Sister Agathe disrobed noiselessly behind her curtains and glided into bed without having revealed, in the faint candlelight, as much as a shadow of herself. Adrienne pattered about the room, shook and folded her garments with great care, placing them on the back of a chair as she had been taught to do when a child at the convent. It secretly pleased Sister Agathe to feel that her dear Adrienne clung to the habits acquired in her youth.

But Adrienne could not sleep. She did not greatly desire to do so. These hours seemed too precious to be cast into the oblivion of slumber.

"Are you not asleep, Adrienne?"

"No, Sister Agathe. You know it is always so the first night. The excitement of my arrival—I don't know what—keeps me awake."

"Say your 'Hail, Mary,' dear child, over and over."

"I have done so, Sister Agathe; it does not help."

"Then lie quite still on your side and think of nothing but your own respiration. I have heard that such inducement to sleep seldom fails."

"I will try. Good night, Sister Agathe."

"Good night, dear child. May the Holy Virgin guard you."

An hour later Adrienne was still lying with wide, wakeful eyes, listening to the regular breathing of Sister Agathe. The trailing of the passing wind through the treetops, the ceaseless babble of the rivulet were some of the sounds that came to her faintly through the night.

The days of the fortnight which followed were in character much like the first peaceful, uneventful day of her arrival, with the exception only that she devoutly heard mass every morning at an early hour in the convent chapel, and on Sundays sang in the choir in her agreeable, cultivated voice, which was heard with delight and the warmest appreciation.

When the day of her departure came, Sister Agathe was not satisfied to say good-bye at the portal as the others did. She walked down the drive beside the creeping old cabriolet, chattering her pleasant last words. And then she stood—it was as far as she might go—at the edge of the road, waving good-bye in response to the fluttering of Adrienne's handkerchief. Four hours later Sister Agathe, who was instructing a class of little girls for their first communion, looked up at the classroom clock and murmured: "Adrienne is at home now."

Yes, Adrienne was at home. Paris had engulfed her.

At the very hour when Sister Agathe looked up at the clock, Adrienne, clad in a charming negligé, was reclining indolently in the depths of a luxurious armchair. The bright room was in its accustomed state of picturesque disorder. Musical scores were scattered upon the open piano. Thrown carelessly over the backs of chairs were puzzling and astonishing-looking garments.

In a large gilded cage near the window perched a clumsy green parrot. He blinked stupidly at a young girl in street dress who was exerting herself to make him talk.

In the center of the room stood Sophie, that thorn in her mistress's side. With hands plunged in the deep pockets of her apron, her white starched cap quivering with each emphatic motion of her grizzled head, she was holding forth, to the evident ennui of the two young women. She was saying:

"Heaven knows I have stood enough in the six years I have been with Mademoiselle; but never such indignities as I have had to endure in the past two weeks at the hands of that man who calls himself a manager! The very first day—and I, good enough to notify him at once of Mademoiselle's flight—he arrives like a lion; I tell you, like a lion. He insists upon knowing Mademoiselle's whereabouts. How can I tell him any more than the statue out there in the square? He calls me a liar! Me, me—a liar! He declares he is ruined. The public will not stand La Petite Gilberta in the role which Mademoiselle has made so famous—La Petite Gilberta, who dances like a jointed wooden figure and sings like a *traînée* of a *café chantant.* If I were to tell La Gilberta that, as I easily might, I guarantee it would not be well for the few straggling hairs which he has left on that miserable head of his!

"What could he do? He was obliged to inform the public that Mademoiselle was ill; and then began my real torment! Answering this one and that one with their cards, their flowers, their dainties in covered dishes! which, I must admit, saved Florine and me much cooking. And all the while having to tell them that the physician had advised for Mademoiselle a rest of two weeks at some watering-place, the name of which I had forgotten!"

Adrienne had been contemplating old Sophie with quizzical, half-closed eyes, and pelting her with hot-house roses which lay in her lap, and which she nipped off short from their graceful stems for that purpose. Each rose struck Sophie full in the face; but they did not disconcert her or once stem the torrent of her talk.

"Oh, Adrienne!" entreated the young girl at the parrot's cage. "Make her hush; please do something. How can you ever expect Zozo to talk? A dozen times he has been on the point of saying something! I tell you, she stupefies him with her chatter."

"My good Sophie," remarked Adrienne, not changing her attitude, "you see the roses are all used up. But I assure you, anything at hand goes," carelessly picking up a book from the table beside her. "What is this? Mons. Zola! Now I warn you, Sophie, the weightiness, the heaviness of Mons. Zola are such that they cannot fail to prostrate you; thankful you may be if they leave you with energy to regain your feet."

"Mademoiselle's pleasantries are all very well; but if I am to be shown the door for it—if I am to be crippled for it—I shall say that I think Mademoiselle is a woman without conscience and without heart. To torture a man as she does! A man? No, an angel!

"Each day he has come with sad visage and drooping mien. 'No news, Sophie?'

" 'None, Monsieur Henri.' 'Have you no idea where she has gone?' 'Not any more than the statue in the square, Monsieur.' 'Is it perhaps possible that she may not return at all?' with his face blanching like that curtain.

"I assure him you will be back at the end of the fortnight. I entreat him to have patience. He drags himself, *désolé*, about the room, picking up Mademoiselle's fan, her gloves, her music, and turning them over and over in his hands. Mademoiselle's slipper, which she took off to throw at me in the impatience of her departure, and which I purposely left lying where it fell on the chiffonier—he kissed it—I saw him do it—and thrust it into his pocket, thinking himself unobserved.

"The same song each day. I beg him to eat a little good soup which I have prepared. 'I cannot eat, my dear Sophie.' The other night he came and stood long gazing out of the window at the stars. When he turned he was wiping his eyes; they were red. He said he had been riding in the dust, which had inflamed them. But I knew better; he had been crying.

"*Ma foi!* in his place I would snap my finger at such cruelty. I would go out and amuse myself. What is the use of being young!"

Adrienne arose with a laugh. She went and seizing old Sophie by the shoulders shook her till the white cap wobbled on her head.

"What is the use of all this litany, my good Sophie? Year after year the same! Have you forgotten that I have come a long, dusty journey by rail, and that I am perishing of hunger and thirst? Bring us a bottle of Château Yquem and a biscuit and my box of cigarettes." Sophie had freed herself, and was retreating toward the door. "And, Sophie! If Monsieur Henri is still waiting, tell him to come up."

It was precisely a year later. The spring had come again, and Paris was intoxicated.

Old Sophie sat in her kitchen discoursing to a neighbor who had come in to borrow some trifling kitchen utensil from the old *bonne*.

"You know, Rosalie, I begin to believe it is an attack of lunacy which seizes her once a year. I wouldn't say it to everyone, but with you I know it will go no further. She ought to be treated for it; a physician should be consulted; it is not well to neglect such things and let them run on.

"It came this morning like a thunder clap. As I am sitting here, there had been no thought or mention of a journey. The baker had come into the kitchen—you know what a gallant he is—with always a girl in his eye. He laid the bread down upon the table and beside it a bunch of lilacs. I didn't know they had bloomed yet. 'For Mam'selle Florine, with my regards,' he said with his foolish simper.

"Now, you know I was not going to call Florine from her work in order to present her the baker's flowers. All the same, it would not do to let them wither. I went with them in my hand into the dining room to get a majolica pitcher which I had put away in the closet there, on an upper shelf, because the handle was broken. Mademoiselle, who rises early, had just come from her bath, and was crossing the hall that opens into the dining room. Just as she was, in her white *peignoir*, she thrust her head into the dining room, snuffling the air and exclaiming, 'What do I smell?'

"She espied the flowers in my hand and pounced upon them

like a cat upon a mouse. She held them up to her, burying her face in them for the longest time, only uttering a long 'Ah!'

" 'Sophie, I am going away. Get out the little black trunk; a few of the plainest garments I have; my brown dress that I have not yet worn.'

" 'But, Mademoiselle,' I protested, 'you forget that you have ordered a breakfast of a hundred francs for tomorrow.'

" 'Shut up!' she cried, stamping her foot.

" 'You forget how the manager will rave,' I persisted, 'and vilify me. And you will go like that without a word of adieu to Monsieur Paul, who is an angel if ever one trod the earth.'

"I tell you, Rosalie, her eyes flamed.

" 'Do as I tell you this instant,' she exclaimed, 'or I will strangle you—with your Monsieur Paul and your manager and your hundred francs!' "

"Yes," affirmed Rosalie, "it is insanity. I had a cousin seized in the same way one morning, when she smelled calf's liver frying with onions. Before night it took two men to hold her."

"I could well see it was insanity, my dear Rosalie, and I uttered not another word as I feared for my life. I simply obeyed her every command in silence. And now—whiff, she is gone! God knows where. But between us, Rosalie—I wouldn't say it to Florine—but I believe it is for no good. I, in Monsieur Paul's place, should have her watched. I would put a detective upon her track.

"Now I am going to close up; barricade the entire establishment. Monsieur Paul, the manager, visitors, all—all may ring and knock and shout themselves hoarse. I am tired of it all. To be vilified and called a liar—at my age, Rosalie!"

Adrienne left her trunk at the small railway station, as the old cabriolet was not at the moment available; and she gladly walked the mile or two of pleasant roadway which led to the convent. How infinitely calm, peaceful, penetrating was the charm of the verdant, undulating country spreading out on all sides of her! She walked along the clear smooth road, twirling her parasol; humming a gay tune; nipping here and there a bud or a waxlike leaf from the hedges along the way; and all the while drinking deep draughts of complacency and content.

She stopped, as she had always done, to pluck lilacs in her path.

As she approached the convent she fancied that a white-capped face had glanced fleetingly from a window; but she must have been mistaken. Evidently she had not been seen, and this time would take them by surprise. She smiled to think how Sister Agathe would utter a little joyous cry of amazement, and in fancy she already felt the warmth and tenderness of the nun's embrace. And how Sister Marceline and the others would laugh, and make game of her puffed sleeves! For puffed sleeves had come into fashion since last year; and the vagaries of fashion always afforded infinite merriment to the nuns. No, they surely had not seen her.

She ascended lightly the stone steps and rang the bell. She could hear the sharp metallic sound reverberate through the halls. Before its last note had died away the door was opened very slightly, very cautiously by a lay sister who stood there with downcast eyes and flaming cheeks. Through the narrow opening she thrust forward toward Adrienne a package and a letter, saying, in confused tones: "By order of our Mother Superior." After which she closed the door hastily and turned the heavy key in the great lock.

Adrienne remained stunned. She could not gather her faculties to grasp the meaning of this singular reception. The lilacs fell from her arms to the stone portico on which she was standing. She turned the note and the parcel stupidly over in her hands, instinctively dreading what their contents might disclose.

The outlines of the crucifix were plainly to be felt through the wrapper of the bundle, and she guessed, without having courage to assure herself, that the jeweled necklace and the altar cloth accompanied it.

Leaning against the heavy oaken door for support, Adrienne opened the letter. She did not seem to read the few bitter reproachful lines word by word—the lines that banished her forever from this haven of peace, where her soul was wont to come and refresh itself. They imprinted themselves as a whole upon her brain, in all their seeming cruelty—she did not dare to say injustice.

There was no anger in her heart; that would doubtless possess her later, when her nimble intelligence would begin to seek out the origin of this treacherous turn. Now, there was only room for tears. She leaned her forehead against the heavy oaken panel of the door and wept with the abandonment of a little child.

She descended the steps with a nerveless and dragging tread. Once as she was walking away, she turned to look back at the imposing façade of the convent, hoping to see a familiar face, or a hand, even, giving a faint token that she was still cherished by some one faithful heart. But she saw only the polished windows looking down at her like so many cold and glittering and reproachful eyes.

In the little white room above the chapel, a woman knelt beside the bed on which Adrienne had slept. Her face was pressed deep in the pillow in her efforts to smother the sobs that convulsed her frame. It was Sister Agathe.

After a short while, a lay sister came out of the door with

a broom, and swept away the lilac blossoms which Adrienne had let fall upon the portico.

"Lilacs." Written May 14–16, 1894. Published in *New Orleans Times-Democrat* (December 20, 1896).

# TI DÉMON
# (A HORSE STORY)

Herminia, mounted upon a dejected-looking sorrel pony, was climbing the gradual slope of a pine hill one morning in summer. She was a 'Cadian girl of the old Bayou Derbanne settlement. The pony was of the variety known indifferently as Indian, Mustang or Texan. Nothing remained of the spirited qualities of his youth. His coat in places was worn away to the hide. In other spots it grew in long tufts and clumps. To the pommel of the saddle was attached an Indian basket containing eggs packed in cotton seed; and beside, the girl carried some garden truck in a coarse bag.

From the moment of leaving her home on the bayou, Herminia had noticed a slight limp in Ti Démon's left fore foot. But, to pay special attention to his peculiarities would have been to encourage him in what she considered an objectionable line of conduct.

"*Allons donc!* You! Ti Démon! W'at's the matter with you?" she exclaimed from time to time. They had long left the bayou road and had penetrated far into the pine forest. The ascent at times was steep and the pony's feet slipped over the pine needles.

"I b'lieve you doin' on purpose!" she exclaimed vexatiously. "If I done right I would walked myse'f f'om the firs' an' lef' you behine." Ti Démon held his leg doubled at a sharp angle and seemed unable to touch it to the ground. At this, Herminia sprang from the saddle, and going forward, lifted the animal's foot to examine it.

The leg was shaggy and might have been swollen; she could not tell. But there was no sign of his having picked up a nail, a stone, or any foreign substance.

"Come 'long, Ti Démon. *Courage!*" and she tried to lead him by the bridle. But he could not be persuaded to move.

The girl stayed wondering what she should do. The horse could go no further; that was a self evident fact. Her own two legs were as sturdy as steel and could carry her many miles. But the question which confronted her was whether she should turn and go back home or whether she should continue on her way to Monsieur Labatier's. The planter had his summer home in the hills where there were neither flies, mosquitoes, fevers, fleas nor any of the trials which often afflict the bayou dwellers in summer.

It was nearer to go to the planter's—not more than three miles. And Herminia cherished the certainty of being well received up there. Madame Labatier would pay her handsomely for the eggs and vegetables. They would invite her to dine and give her a sip of wine. She would have an opportunity of observing the toilets and manners of the young ladies—two nieces who were spending a month in the hills. But above all there would be young Mr. Prospère Labatier who perhaps would say:

"Ah! Herminia, it is too bad! Allow me to len' you my ho'se to return home," or else:

"Will you permit me the pleasure of escorting you home in my buggy?" These last considerations determined Herminia beyond further hesitancy.

With the piece of rope which she carried on such occasions she tied Ti Démon to a pine tree near the sandy road in a pleasant, shady spot.

"Now, stay there, till I come back. It's yo' own fault if you got to go hungry. You can't expec' me to tote you on my back, *grosse bête!*" She patted him kindly and turning her back upon him, proceeded to ascend the hill with a little springy step. She wore a calico dress of vivid red and a white sun bonnet from whose depths twinkled two black eyes, quick as a squirrel's.

Ti Démon observed her with his dull eyes and continued to hold his foot from the ground like a veritable martyr. It was still and restful in the forest and if Ti Démon had not been suffering acutely, he would have enjoyed the peaceful moment. Patches of sunlight played upon his back; a couple of red ants crawled up his hind leg; he slowly swished his long, scant tail. The mocking birds began to sing a duet in the top of a pine tree. They were young; they could sing and rejoice; they knew nothing of the tribulations attending upon old age. Ti Démon thought to himself:

"If this thing keeps up, there's no telling where it will land me."

While he understood Herminia's broken English and her

mother's 'Cadian French, Ti Démon always thought in his native language, that he had imbibed in his youth in the Indian Nation.

He stood for some hours very still listening to the drowsy noises of the forest. Then a blessed relaxation began to invade the afflicted foreleg. The pain perceptibly died away, and he straightened the limb without difficulty. Ti Démon uttered a deep sigh of relief. But with the consciousness of returning comfort came the realization of his unpleasant situation. He could fancy nothing more uninteresting than to be fastened thus to a tree in the heart of the pine forest. He already began to grow hungry in anticipation of the hunger which would assail him later. He had no means of knowing what hour Herminia would return and release him from his sad predicament. It was then that Ti Démon put into practice one of his chief accomplishments. He began deliberately to unknot the rope with his old, yellow teeth. He had observed Herminia give it an extra knot and had even heard her say:

"There! if you undo that, Ti Démon, they'll have to allow you got mo' sense than Raymond's mule." The remark had offended him. He hated the constant association with Raymond's mule to which he was subjected.

He managed after persistent effort to untie the knot, and Ti Démon soon found himself free to roam withersoever he chose. If he had been a dog he would have turned his nose uphill and followed in the footsteps of his mistress. But he was only a pony of rather low breeding and almost wholly devoid of sentiment.

Ti Démon walked leisurely down the slope, following the path by which he had come. It was a pleasing diversion to be thus permitted to roam at will. He did not linger however to nibble here and there after the manner of stray horses for he knew well that the pine hill afforded little sustenance to man or beast; and he preferred to wait and whet his appetite with the luscious bits that grew below along the bayou. He appeared like a wise old philosopher plunged in thought.

By frequent stepping upon the rope dangling from his neck, it at length gave way, much to Ti Démon's satisfaction.

"Now! if I could get rid of the saddle as easily!" thought he.

It was impossible to reach the girt with his teeth; he tried that. Then Ti Démon shook himself till his coat bristled; he rubbed himself against the tree; he rolled over on his side, on his back, but the only result which he reached was to turn the saddle so that it dangled beneath him as he walked. At this he swore lustily to himself, as his master, Blanco Bill used to swear so many years back in the Nation. He did not feel now like nibbling grass or amusing himself in any way. His one thought was to get home to his dinner of soft food and be rid of the hateful encumbrance beating against his legs.

When Ti Démon found himself standing before his home, he viewed the situation with sullen disapproval. The little house was closed and silent. The only living thing to be seen was the cat sleeping in the shade of the gallery. A line of yellow pumpkins gleamed along the boards in the sun. There was a hoe leaning up against the fence where Herminia's mother who had been hoeing the tobacco plants had left it.

"Just as I thought," grumbled Ti Démon. "I could 'a sworn to it. That woman's off galavanting down the river again; dropped her hoe the minute Herminia's back was turned. An' them kids ought to be back from school; drat 'em! A thousand dollars to a doughnut they gone crawfishing. If I don't shake this whole shootin' match first chance I get, my name ain't Spitfire." It was the name Blanco Bill had given him at birth and the only one he acknowledged officially.

"There's no opening gates or lifting latches or anything since they got them newfangled padlocks on," he further reflected, "if there was, I'd get inside there an' them cabbages an' cow-peas 'ld be nuts for me. Reckon I'll stroll down an' see if I c'n ketch Solistan at home." Ti Démon turned again to the road and with a deliberate stride which sent the saddle bumping and thumping, he headed for the neighboring farm up the bayou.

There was nothing startling to Solistan in seeing Ti Démon staring over his fence. He simply thought Herminia had returned from the pine hill, that the animal had got loose from the "lot" and he went forward to drive him into his own enclosure, intending to take him home later, when he should be at leisure.

But Solistan's astonishment was acute when he discovered Ti Démon's condition; covered with clay and bits of sticks and bark, Herminia's saddle hanging beneath him, and the blanket gone. It was but the work of a moment to drive the pony back in the lot; to throw a measure of corn into the trough; to saddle his own horse and start off at a mad gallop.

"Wonder what all the commotion's about," thought Ti Démon as he attempted to munch the corn from the cob. "He didn't take much trouble to pick an' choose when he gave me this mess. This here corn mus' be a hundred years old; or my teeth ain't what they used to be."

Solistan knew Ti Démon too well to believe that he had cut any capers which could have resulted in harm to Herminia. But the saddle must have turned with her; he might have stumbled and thrown her. A hundred misgivings assailed him, especially after he had been to her house and discovered the place deserted by all save the cat asleep in the shade of the gallery.

Solistan had started away just as he was, in his blue checked shirt and his boots heavy with the damp earth of the fields. He never dreamt of stopping to make a bit of toilet. He could not remember when he had in his life been a prey to such uneasiness. He had known and liked Herminia all her life; but she was always there at hand, seeming to be a natural part of the surroundings to which he was accustomed. It was only at that moment, when the menace of some dreadful and unknown fate hung over her, that he fully realized the depth and nature of his attachment for the girl.

Solistan rode far into the forest, his anxiety growing at every moment, and sick with dread of what any turn or bend in the road might reveal to him. He could not contain himself. He shouted for joy when he saw Herminia standing unharmed and motionless beneath a tall pine tree, as though she were holding a conversation and even some argument with his rugged majesty.

Her sunbonnet hung on her arm and her whole attitude was one of deep dejection. Herminia was in truth helplessly surveying the spot where she had so insecurely fastened Ti Démon, who had disappeared, leaving not so much as a hair of his hide or tail to say that he had ever been there. This seeming treachery on the part of Ti Démon marked the culmination of Herminia's mortification, and the tears were suffocating her.

Oh! it had been very fine up at the planter's! Too fine indeed. There was a large house-party congregated for the day, and little Herminia standing on the back gallery with her eggs and garden truck had been scarcely noticed.

She had been permitted to dine with them, wedged in between two stout old people; but she felt like an intruder and even perceived that the servants gave themselves the air of forgetting her. The young ladies' volubility and ease of manner made her feel small and insignificant; and their fluffy summer toilets conveyed to her only the bitter conviction of never being able to reproduce in calico such intricacy of ruffles and puffs. As for Mr. Prospère, he had only exclaimed: "Hello! Herminia!" in passing hastily along the gallery when she sat with her garden truck and eggs.

She could scarcely eat, for mortification and disappointment. She had not had an opportunity of relating the misadventure to her pony, and when, at leaving, the planter solicitously asked how she was going to get home, Herminia replied with forced dignity that she had left her horse tied a little below in the woods.

There was the wood all right, and there was Herminia, but where was the pony? That was the question which Herminia seemed to be asking of the big pine tree when Solistan rode up in such hot haste and flung himself from the saddle as if to reach out for some prize that he had pursued and captured.

"Oh! Solistan! I lef' Ti Démon fasten' yere this mornin'; he couldn' walk; an' now he's gone! Oh! Solistan! Someone mus' 'ave stole' 'im!"

"Ti Démon is in my lot eatin' co'n fo' all he's worth. The saddle was turned under 'im. I thought you'd got hurt." Solistan wiped his steaming, beaming face with his bandanna; and Herminia felt at beholding him that she had never been so glad or thankful to see any one in her life. And she could not think of any one whom she would rather have seen at that moment; not even Mr. Prospère. Not even if he had come along and said:

"Allow me the pleasure of escorting you home in my buggy, Herminia!"

Solistan's was a big, broadbacked horse, and Herminia sat very comfortably behind the young man on her way back to the bayou; holding on to his suspenders when the occasion required it.

After they had reached Solistan's home and he had brought forth Ti Démon resaddled and refreshed, the following bit of conversation took place between them. Herminia was mounted, ready to start, and Solistan was still holding the animal's bridle.

"That Ti Démon of yo's is played out, Herminia. He isn't safe, I tell you. He'll play you a mean trick some these days. I been thinkin' you better use that li'l mare I traded with Raul fo' las' spring."

"Oh! Solistan! it would take too much corn to feed 'im. We got Raymond's mule to feed; an' Ti Démon eats fo' three, him—"

"Oh! shoot Ti Démon; his time's over."

"Shoot Ti Démon!" cried the girl, flushing with indignation. "You talkin' like crazy, Solistan. I would soon think o' takin' a gun an' shootin' someone passin' 'long the road."

"I'm jus' talkin'," laughed Solistan, perceiving the impression which his heartless remark had produced. "Ole Démon's good fo' a long time yet. He's plenty good to haul water or tote the children up an' down the bayou road. But don't you ever trus' yo'se'f in the woods with 'im again."

"You c'n be sho' of that, Solistan."

"An' 'bout feedin'," he went on, greatly occupied with the buckle of Ti Démon's bridle, "I could keep on feedin' the ho'se, an' if that plan don't suit you, w'at you think 'bout takin' me 'long with the ho'se, Herminia?"

"Takin' you, Solistan!"

"W'y not? We plenty ole 'nough; you mus' be mos' eighteen, an' I'm goin' on twenty-three, me."

"I better be goin'. We c'n talk 'bout that 'nother time."

"W'en, Herminia! W'en?" implored Solistan holding on to the bridle of her pony, "tonight if I come down yonder? Say, tonight?"

"Oh Solistan, le' me go!"

"An' w'at will you tell me, Herminia?"

"We'll see 'bout that," she laughed over her shoulder as Ti Démon started away with a stiff trot.

But all the joy of life had forever left the breast of Ti Démon. Solistan's sinister remarks had made a deep and painful impression which he could not rid himself of.

When, in the autumn following, the young farmer took Herminia home to be his wife, and also took Ti Démon with the benevolent intention of feeding him all the rest of his life, it was then that Ti Démon's days were given over to brooding upon the possible fate which awaited him.

Once in an unguarded moment, Ti Démon walked himself off, across Bayou Derbanne, along the Sabine and away from the haunts which had known him so long.

"If there's goin' to be any shootin'," reflected Ti Démon as he limped along, swishing his tail, "it's time fo' me to be pullin' my freight."

It was during the winter following that Solistan one evening said to his wife as she bent over the fire, getting their evening meal.

"W'at you think, Herminia? Raul tole me w'en he was drivin' his drove of cattle into Texas las' month, they came 'cross Ti Démon layin' dead in the Bonham road. The li'le rascal mus' a' been on his way to the Indian Nation."

"Oh! Po' Ti Démon!" exclaimed Herminia holding aloft the huge spoon with which she had been stirring the *couche-couche*. "He was a good an' faithful ho'se! yes!"

"That's true, Herminia," replied Solistan with philosophic resignation, "but who knows! maybe it is all fo' the best!"

"A Horse Story." Written March 1898, with the title "Ti Démon." First published in *A Kate Chopin Miscellany* (1979).

# TI DÉMON

"It's this way," said Ti Démon to Aristides Bonneau—"If I go yonda with you to Symond's sto', it'll be half pas' eight befo' I git out to Marianne an' she'll sho' be gone to bed—an' she won' know how come I missed goin'."

Every Saturday afternoon Ti Démon, as did many others along the 'Cadian Bayou, laid aside hoe and plow—turned the mule loose and all primped up—*endimanché* as they say down there—betook himself to town on his ragged pony, his one luxury. After putting the pony in the lot adjoining Gamarché's store—he would go about town making his necessary purchases, gazing in at the windows, finally picking up a ribbon or a cornet of candy for his Marianne. At half past six he invariably betook himself to Marianne's who lived with her mother a little beyond the outskirts of town. She was his fiancée. He was going to marry her at the close of summer when the crops were gathered, and he was happy in a certain unemotional way that took things for granted.

His name was Plaisance, but his mother called him Ti Démon when he was a baby and kept her awake bawling at night, and the name stuck to him. It had lost all significance, however, in his growing goodness, and in the bovine mildness that characterized his youth years the name identified itself with his personality and became almost a synonym for gentleness.

At half past six, instead of being out at Marianne's, he was lounging in the drug store where he had allowed himself to be persuaded into a rendez-vouz with Aristides. He was a square clumsy fellow with sunburnt hair and skin—features that were not bad and eyes that were decidedly good as they reflected a peaceful soul. Gazing down into the show case of the drug store, Ti Démon longed to be rich, more on Marianne's account than his own for the things arrayed before him were such as appealed distinctly to the feminine taste—green and yellow perfumes in bottles—hand mirrors—toilet powders—savon fin—dainty writing paper—a hundred costly nothings which the Druggist had little hope or chance of selling before Christmas. Ti Démon felt that a bale of cotton would hardly more than cover the price of a full and free and reckless indulgence—of the longings which assailed him through Marianne as he gazed down into the drug-store showcase.

Aristides soon joined him and together they left the store and walked down the main street of the town, across the footbridge that covered a deep ravine and down the hill toward a motley group of shanties—one of which was Symond's store, not so much a store as a resort for young men whose erratic inclinations sometimes led them to seek more spirited diversion than the domestic and social circle offered them. Perhaps no other man in town could so have tempted and prevailed with Ti Démon. It flattered his self-complacency to be seen walking down the street with Aristides whose distinction of manner was unquestionable, whose grace and amiability made him an object of envy with the men and a creature to be worshiped by susceptible women. By contrast Ti Démon was all the more conscious of his own lurching plowman's walk, his awkward stoop and broad heavy hands that looked as if they might do the office of sledge hammers if occasion required.

The foul-smelling coal-oil lamps had been lighted in Symond's back room when they reached there. Several men were already gathered playing cards around rude tables whose grimy tops bore the stale and fresh marks of liquor glasses. Aristides and Ti Démon had strolled down for a social game of seven-up and a convivial hour among friends and acquaintances. For the young farmer had expressed a determination to leave at 8 o'clock and rejoin Marianne who he knew would be wondering and perhaps grieving at his absence. But at 8 o'clock Ti Démon was more excited than he had ever been in his life. His big fist was coming down on the table with a reckless disregard for the fate of the jingling glasses and his big horse laugh, mellowed by numerous toddies, resounded and stirred a pleasing animation about him. The game of seven-up had been changed to poker. Ti Démon formed one of the seven men at his table, and though he was acquainted with the game, having played on rare occasions, never before had the fluctuations of the game so excited him. It was the hoarse tones of the clock in the store adjoining, striking 10 that brought him partially to his senses and reminded him of his disregarded intentions. "Leave me out this time, I got to go," said Ti Démon rising, conscious of stiffened joints. "I ain't winnin' and I ain't losin' to talk about, so it don't make no difference. Where's my hat—w'at become o' Mr. Aristides?"

"W'ere yo' sense, Ti Démon, Aristides lef' a couple hours ago—he tole you he was goin' and you didn' pay any attention.

Yo' hat's on yo' head w'ere it ought to be. Deal them cards over again—you dealt a han' to Ti Démon, it's goin' to spoil the draw. I'm glad he's gone—he makes mo' noise than Symond's donkey—"

Ti Démon managed to get out on the gallery with a great clatter of brogans and overturning of chairs. He was clumsy and noisy. Once out of doors, he drew a deep long breath of the fresh spring night. Looking across the hollow and far up the opposite slope he could see a light in the window of Marianne's house. He vaguely wondered if she had gone to bed. He vaguely hoped she might be still sitting out on the gallery with her mother. The night was so beautiful that it might well tempt any one to steal a few hours from sleep, and linger out under the sky to taste the delight of it. He left the shanty and started off in the direction of Marianne's cottage. He was conscious of some unsteadiness of gait. He knew he was not entirely sober but was confident of his ability to disguise that fact from Marianne, if he should be fortunate enough to find her still up. He was seized as he had never been in his life before, by a flood of tenderness, a conscious longing for the girl that he had been brought to fully realize perhaps by his moment of weakness and disloyalty, perhaps as much by the subtle spirit of the caressing night, the soft effulgence the moon was shedding over the country, the poignant odors of the spring. The good familiar scent of new plowed earth assailed him and made him think of his big field on the bayou—of his home—and Marianne, as she would be, at picking time, coming down between the tall rows of white bursting cotton to meet him. The thought was like a vivid picture flashed and imprinted upon his brain. It was so sweet a thought that he would not give it up, but kept it with him in his walk and treasured it and fondled it.

Then up the slope stood the poor little cottage a good bit

back from the road. It was an upward, grassy road with a few faint wagon tracks. There was a row of trees at irregular intervals along the fence, and they cast deep shadows across the white moonlight. Ascending the road, Ti Démon saw two people approaching—advancing toward him—walking slowly arm in arm. At first he did not recognize them, passing slowly in and out, in and out of the shadows. But when they stopped in the moonlight to pick some white blossoms hanging over the fence, he knew them. It was Aristides and Marianne. The young man fixed a white spray in the girl's heavy black braids. He seemed to linger over the pleasing task, then arm in arm they resumed their walk—continued to approach Ti Démon. With the first flash of recognition came madness. As vividly as the powerful picture of love and domestic peace had imprinted upon his mind—just as sharply now came in a blinding flash the conviction of trickery and deceit. Marianne, not devoid of coquetry, could see no harm in accepting the attentions of Aristides or any other agreeable youth in the absence of her fiancé. It was with no feeling of guiltiness that she perceived him approaching. On the contrary, she framed a reproach in her mind and uttered it as he came near—"You takin' yo' time to night, I mus' say, Ti Démon." But with an utter disregard for her words—a terrible purpose in his newly aroused consciousness, in speechless wrath he tore her companion from her side and fell upon him with those big broad fists that could do the service of sledge hammers when occasion required.

"You crazy! Ti Démon! Help—*Au secours—au secours*—you crazy—Ti Démon," shrieked Marianne hanging upon him in fear and desperation.

There was hardly a shred of soul left in Aristides's shapely body when help came—negroes running from near cabins at the sound of Marianne's screams. The force of numbers against him alone prevailed with Ti Démon to desist in his deadly work. He left Marianne bruised and weeping, Aristides battered and bleeding, lying unconscious on the ground in the moonlight, and the negroes all standing there in helpless indecision—and he went limping away—down the slope across the hollow over the footbridge that crossed the ravine and back into town. He took his pony from the lot where he had left it, mounted and rode in a gentle canter back to his home on the 'Cadian Bayou.

Of course Marianne never viewed him after that—she would not trust her life in the keeping of so murderous a madman. Nor did she marry Aristides, who in truth never had any intention of asking her. But a girl with so sweet a manner, with tender eyes and dark and glossy braids had but the trouble of choosing among the 'Cadian youths along the bayou. That was Ti Démon's one and only demoniacal outburst during his life, but it affected the community in an inexplicable way. Some one said that Aristides said he was going to shoot Ti Démon at sight. So Ti Démon got permission to carry a pistol—a rusty old blunderbuss that was a sore trial and inconvenience for so peaceable a man to lug around with him. Aristides, whatever he might have said, had no intention of molesting him—he never prosecuted his assailant as he might have done, and even got into a way of turning up one street when he saw Ti Démon coming down the other. "He's a dangerous man, that 'Cadian," said Aristides; "mark my words, he'll kill his man befo' he's through." The negroes who had been witnesses to the encounter on the moonlit slope described it in language that made children and timid women shriek and tremble and made men look to their firearms. As for Marianne she always begged to be spared describing the horror of it. People began to believe he had been well named after all—"*il est bien nommé Ti Démon, va!*" said women to each other.

"You can't fool with Ti Démon—he don' say much, him, but w'en he gits mad, mine out!" It somehow got into the air and stayed there—other men fought and brawled and bled and quietly resumed their roles of law-abiding citizens—not so with Ti Démon. Little children got into the way of scrambling into the house when they saw him coming. Years later he was sometimes pointed out to strangers by those of a younger generation who had no distinctive idea of the nature of his crimes. "You see that ol' fellow—he's bad as they make 'em—he's dangerous him—they call 'm Ti Démon."

"Ti Démon." Written November 1899. First published in *The Complete Works of Kate Chopin* (1969).

# THE GODMOTHER

## I

Tante Elodie attracted youth in some incomprehensible way. It was seldom there was not a group of young people gathered about her fire in winter or sitting with her in summer, in the pleasant shade of the live-oaks that screened the gallery.

There were several persons forming a half circle around her generous chimney early one evening in February. There were Madame Nicolas's two tiny little girls who sat on the floor and played with a cat the whole time; Madame Nicolas herself, who only came for the little girls and insisted on hurrying away because it was time to put the children to bed, and who, moreover, was expecting a caller. There was a fair, blonde girl, one of the younger teachers at the Normal school. Gabriel

Lucaze offered to escort her home when she got up to go, after Madame Nicolas's departure. But she had already accepted the company of a silent, studious looking youth who had come there in the hope of meeting her. So they all went away but young Gabriel Lucaze, Tante Elodie's godson, who stayed and played cribbage with her. They played at a small table on which were a shaded lamp, a few magazines and a dish of *pralines* which the lady took great pleasure in nibbling during the reflective pauses of the game. They had played one game and were nearing the end of the second. He laid a queen upon the table.

"Fifteen-two" she said, playing a five.

"Twenty, and a pair."

"Twenty-five. Six points for me."

"Its a 'go.' "

"Thirty-one and out. That is the second game I've won. Will you play another rubber, Gabriel?"

"Not much, Tante Elodie, when you are playing in such luck. Besides, I've got to get out, it's half-past-eight." He had played recklessly, often glancing at the bronze clock which reposed majestically beneath its crystal globe on the mantlepiece. He prepared at once to leave, going before the gilt-framed, oval mirror to fold and arrange a silk muffler beneath his great coat.

He was rather good looking. That is, he was healthy looking; his face a little florid, and hair almost black. It was short and curly and parted on one side. His eyes were fine when they were not bloodshot, as they sometimes were. His mouth might have been better. It was not disagreeable or unpleasant, but it was unsatisfactory and drooped a little at the corners. However, he was good to look at as he crossed the muffler over his chest. His face was unusually alert. Tante Elodie looked at him in the glass.

"Will you be warm enough, my boy? It has turned very cold since six o'clock."

"Plenty warm. Too warm."

"Where are you going?"

"Now, Tante Elodie," he said, turning, and laying a hand on her shoulder; he was holding his soft felt hat in the other. "It is always 'where are you going?' 'Where have you been?' I have spoiled you. I have told you too much. You expect me to tell you everything; consequently, I must sometimes tell you fibs. I am going to confession. There! are you satisfied?" and he bent down and gave her a hearty kiss.

"I am satisfied, provided you go to the right priestess to confession; not up the hill, mind you!"

"Up the hill" meant up at the Normal school with Tante Elodie. She was a very conservative person. "The Normal" seemed to her an unpardonable innovation, with its teachers from Minnesota, from Iowa, from God-knows-where, bringing strange ways and manners to the old town. She was one, also, who considered the emancipation of slaves a great mistake. She had many reasons for thinking so and was often called upon to enumerate this in her wordy arguments with her many opponents.

## II

Tante Elodie distinctly heard the Doctor leave the Widow Nicolas's at a quarter past ten. He visited the handsome and attractive young woman two evenings in the week and always left at the same hour. Tante Elodie's double glass doors opened upon the wide upper gallery. Around the angle of the gallery were the apartments of Madame Nicolas. Any one visiting the widow was obliged to pass Tante Elodie's door. Beneath was a store occasionally occupied by some merchant or other, but oftener vacant. A stairway led down from the porch to the yard where two enormous live-oaks grew and cast a dense shade upon the gallery above, making it an agreeable retreat and resting place on hot summer afternoons. The high, wooden yard-gate opened directly upon the street.

A half hour went by after the Doctor passed her door. Tante Elodie played "solitaire." Another half hour followed and still Tante Elodie was not sleepy nor did she think of going to bed. It was very near midnight when she began to prepare her night toilet and to cover the fire.

The room was very large with heavy rafters across the ceiling. There was an enormous bed over in the corner; a four-posted mahogany covered with a lace spread which was religiously folded every night and laid on a chair. There were some old ambrotypes and photographs about the room; a few comfortable but simple rocking chairs and a broad fire place in which a big log sizzled. It was an attractive room for anyone, not because of anything that was in it except Tante Elodie herself. She was far past fifty. Her hair was still soft and brown and her eyes bright and vivacious. Her figure was slender and nervous. There were many lines in her face, but it did not look care-worn. Had she her youthful flesh, she would have looked very young.

Tante Elodie had spent the evening in munching *pralines* and reading by lamp-light some old magazines that Gabriel Lucaze had brought her from the club.

There was a romance connected with her early days. Romances serve but to feed the imagination of the young; they add nothing to the sum of truth. No one realized this fact more strongly than Tante Elodie herself. While she tacitly condoned the romance, perhaps for the sake of the sympathy it bred, she never thought of Justin Lucaze but with a feeling of gratitude towards the memory of her parents who had prevented her marrying him thirty-five years before. She could have no connection between her deep and powerful affection for young Gabriel Lucaze and her old-time, brief passion for his father. She loved the boy above everything on earth. There was none so attractive to her as he; none so thoughtful of her pleasures and pains. In his devotion there was no trace of a duty-sense; it was the spontaneous expression of affection and seeming dependence.

After Tante Elodie had turned down her bed and undressed, she drew a gray flannel *peignoir* over her nightgown and knelt down to say her prayers; kneeling before a rocker with her bare feet turned to the fire. Prayers were no trifling matter with her. Besides those which she knew by heart, she read litanies and invocations from a book and also a chapter of "The Following of Christ." She had said her *Notre Père*, her *Salve Marie* and *Je crois en Dieu* and was deep in the litany of the Blessed Virgin when she fancied she heard footsteps on the stairs. The night was breathlessly still; it was very late.

"*Vierge des Vierges: Priez pour nous. Mère de Dieu: Priez*—"

Surely there was a stealthy step upon the gallery, and now a hand at her door, striving to lift the latch. Tante Elodie was not afraid. She felt the utmost security in her home and had no dread of mischievous intruders in the peaceful old town. She simply realized that there was some one at her door and that she must find out who it was and what they wanted. She got up from her knees, thrust her feet into her slippers that were near the fire and, lowering the lamp by which she had been reading her litanies, approached the door. There was the very softest rap upon the pane. Tante Elodie unbolted and opened the door the least bit.

"*Qui est là?*" she asked.

"Gabriel." He forced himself into the room before she had time to fully open the door to him.

## III

Gabriel strode past her towards the fire, mechanically taking off his hat, and sat down in the rocker before which she had been kneeling. He sat on the prayer books she had left there. He removed them and laid them upon the table. Seeming to realize in a dazed way that it was not their accustomed place, he threw the two books on a nearby chair.

Tante Elodie raised the lamp and looked at him. His eyes were bloodshot, as they were when he drank or experienced any unusual emotion or excitement. But he was pale and his mouth drooped excessively, and twitched with the effort he made to control it. The top button was wrenched from his coat and his muffler was disarranged. Tante Elodie was grieved to the soul, seeing him thus. She thought he had been drinking.

"Gabriel, w'at is the matter?" she asked imploringly. "Oh, my poor child, w'at is the matter?" He looked at her in a fixed way and passed a hand over his head. He tried to speak, but his voice failed, as with one who experiences stage fright. Then he articulated, hoarsely, swallowing nervously between the slow words:

"I—killed a man—about an hour ago—yonder in the old Nigger-Luke Cabin." Tante Elodie's two hands went suddenly down to the table and she leaned heavily upon them for support.

"You did not; you did not," she panted. "You are drinking. You do not know w'at you are saying. Tell me, Gabriel, who 'as been making you drink? Ah! they will answer to me! You do not know w'at you are saying. *Boute!* how can you know!"

She clutched him and the torn button that hung in the button-hole fell to the floor.

"I don't know why it happened," he went on, gazing into the fire with unseeing eyes, or rather with eyes that saw what was pictured in his mind and not what was before them.

"I've been in cutting scrapes and shooting scrapes that never amounted to anything, when I was just as crazy mad as I was to-night. But I tell you, Tante Elodie, he's dead. I've got to get away. But how are you going to get out of a place like this, when every dog and cat"—His effort had spent itself, and he began to tremble with a nervous chill; his teeth chattered and his lips could not form an utterance.

Tante Elodie, stumbling rather than walking, went over to a small buffet and pouring some brandy into a glass, gave it to him. She took a little herself. She looked much older in the *peignoir* and the handkerchief tied around her head. She sat down beside Gabriel and took his hand. It was cold and clammy.

"Tell me everything," she said with determination, "everything; without delay; and do not speak so loud. We shall see what must be done. Was it a negro? Tell me everything."

"No, it was a white man, you don't know, from Conshotta, named Everson. He was half drunk; a hulking bully as strong as an ox, or I could have licked him. He tortured me until I was frantic. Did you ever see a cat torment a mouse? The mouse can't do anything but lose its head. I lost my head, but I had my knife; that big hornhandled knife."

"Where is it?" she asked sharply. He felt his back pocket.

"I don't know." He did not seem to care, or to realize the importance of the loss.

"Go on; make haste; tell me the whole story. You went from here—you went—go on."

"I went down the river a piece," he said, throwing himself

back in the chair and keeping his eyes fixed upon one burning ember on the hearth, "down to Symund's store where there was a game of cards. A lot of the fellows were there. I played a little and didn't drink anything, and stopped at ten. I was going"—He leaned forward with his elbows on his knees and his hands hanging between. "I was going to see a woman at eleven o'clock; it was the only time I could see her. I came along and when I got by the old Nigger-Luke Cabin I lit a match and looked at my watch. It was too early and it wouldn't do to hang around. I went into the cabin and started a blaze in the chimney with some fine wood I found there. My feet were cold and I sat on an empty soap-box before the fire to dry them. I remember I kept looking at my watch. It was twenty-five minutes to eleven when Everson came into the cabin. He was half drunk and his face was red and looked like a beast. He had left the game and had followed me. I hadn't spoken of where I was going. But he said he knew I was off for a lark and he wanted to go along. I said he couldn't go where I was going, and there was no use talking. He kept it up. At a quarter to eleven I wanted to go, and he went and stood in the doorway.

" 'If I don't go, you don't go', he said, and he kept it up. When I tried to pass him he pushed me back like I was a feather. He didn't get mad. He laughed all the time and drank whiskey out of a bottle he had in his pocket. If I hadn't got mad and lost my head, I might have fooled him or played some trick on him—if I had used my wits. But I didn't know any more what I was doing than the day I threw the inkstand at old Dainean's head when he switched me and made fun of me before the whole school.

"I stooped by the fire and looked at my watch; he was talking all kinds of foulishness I can't repeat. It was eleven o'clock. I was in a killing rage and made a dash for the door. His big body and his big arm were there like an iron bar, and he laughed. I took out my knife and stuck it into him. I don't believe he knew at first that I had touched him, for he kept on laughing; then he fell over like a pig, and the old cabin shook."

Gabriel had raised his clinched hand with an intensely dramatic movement when he said, "I stuck it into him." Then he let his head fall back against the chair and finished the concluding sentences of his story with closed eyes.

"How do you know he is dead?" asked Tante Elodie, whose voice sounded hard and monotonous.

"I only walked ten steps away and went back to see. He was dead. Then I came here. The best thing is to go give myself up, I reckon, and tell the whole story like I've told you. That's about the best thing I can do if I want any peace of mind."

"Are you crazy, Gabriel! You have not yet regained your senses. Listen to me. Listen to me and try to understand what I say."

Her face was full of a hard intelligence he had not seen there before; all the soft womanliness had for the moment faded out of it.

"You 'ave not killed the man Everson," she said deliberately. "You know nothing about 'im. You do not know that he left Symund's or that he followed you. You left at ten o'clock. You came straight in town, not feeling well. You saw a light in my window, came here; rapped on the door; I let you in and gave you something for cramps in the stomach and made you warm yourself and lie down on the sofa. Wait a moment. Stay still there."

She got up and went shuffling out the door, around the angle of the gallery and tapped on Madame Nicolas's door. She could hear the young woman jump out of bed bewildered, asking, "Who is there? Wait! What is it?"

"It is Tante Elodie." The door was unbolted at once.

"Oh! how I hate to trouble you, *chérie*. Poor Gabriel 'as been at my room for hours with the most severe cramps. Nothing I can do seems to relieve 'im. Will you let me 'ave the morphine which Doctor left with you for old Betsy's rheumatism? Ah! thank you. I think a quarter of a grain will relieve 'im. Poor boy! Such suffering! I am so sorry dear, to disturb you. Do not stand by the door, you will take cold. Good night."

Tante Elodie persuaded Gabriel, if the club were still open, to look in there on his way home. He had a room in a relative's house. His mother was dead and his father lived on a plantation several miles from town. Gabriel feared that his nerve would fail him. But Tante Elodie had him up again with a glass of brandy. She said that he must get the fact lodged in his mind that he was innocent. She inspected the young man carefully before he went away, brushing and arranging his toilet. She sewed the missing button on his coat. She had noticed some blood upon his right hand. He himself had not seen it. With a wet towel she washed his face and hands as though he were a little child. She brushed his hair and sent him away with a thousand reiterated precautions.

## IV

Tante Elodie was not overcome in any way after Gabriel left her. She did not indulge in a hysterical moment, but set about accomplishing some purpose which she had evidently had in her mind. She dressed herself again; quickly, nervously, but with much precision. A shawl over her head and a long, black cape across her shoulders made her look like a nun. She quitted her room. It was very dark and very still out of doors. There was only a whispering wail among the live-oak leaves.

Tante Elodie stole noiselessly down the steps and out the

gate. If she had met anyone, she intended to say she was suffering with toothache and was going to the doctor or druggist for relief.

But she met not a soul. She knew every plank, every uneven brick of the sidewalk; every rut of the way, and might have walked with her eyes closed. Strangely enough she had forgotten to pray. Prayer seemed to belong to her moments of contemplation; while now she was all action; prompt, quick, decisive action.

It must have been near upon two o'clock. She did not meet a cat or a dog on her way to the Nigger-Luke Cabin. The hut was well out of town and isolated from a group of tumbled-down shanties some distance off, in which a lazy set of negroes lived. There was not the slightest feeling of fear or horror in her breast. There might have been, had she not already been dominated and possessed by the determination that Gabriel must be shielded from ignominy—maybe, worse.

She glided into the low cabin like a shadow, hugging the side of the open door. She would have stumbled over the dead man's feet if she had not stepped so cautiously. The embers were burning so low that they gave but a faint glow in the sinister cabin with its obscure corners, its black, hanging cobwebs and the dead man lying twisted as he had fallen with his face on his arm.

Once in the cabin the woman crept towards the body on her hands and knees. She was looking for something in the dusky light; something she could not find. Crawling towards the fire over the uneven, creaking boards, she stirred the embers the least bit with a burnt stick that had fallen to one side. She dared not make a blaze. Then she dragged herself once more towards the lifeless body. She pictured how the knife had been thrust in; how it had fallen from Gabriel's hand; how the man had come down like a felled ox. Yes, the knife could not be far off, but she could not discover a trace of it. She slipped her fingers beneath the body and felt all along. The knife lay up under his arm pit. Her hand scraped his chin as she withdrew it. She did not mind. She was exultant at getting the knife. She felt like some other being, possessed by Satan. Some fiend in human shape, some spirit of murder. A cricket began to sing on the hearth.

Tante Elodie noticed the golden gleam of the murdered man's watch chain, and a sudden thought invaded her. With deft, though unsteady fingers, she unhooked the watch and chain. There was money in his pockets. She emptied them, turning the pockets inside out. It was difficult to reach his left hand pockets, but she did so. The money, a few bank notes and some silver coins, together with the watch and knife she tied in her handkerchief. Then she hurried away, taking a long stride across the man's body in order to reach the door.

The stars were like shining pieces of gold upon dark velvet. So Tante Elodie thought as she looked up at them an instant.

There was the sound of disorderly voices away off in the negro shanties. Clasping the parcel close to her breast she began to run. She ran, ran, as fast as some fleet fourfooted creature, ran, panting. She never stopped till she reached the gate that let her in under the live-oaks. The most intent listener could not have heard her as she mounted the stairs; as she let herself in at the door; as she bolted it. Once in the room she began to totter. She was sick to her stomach and her head swam. Instinctively she reached out towards the bed, and fell fainting upon it, face downward.

The gray light of dawn was coming in at her windows. The lamp on the table had burned out. Tante Elodie groaned as she tried to move. And again she groaned with mental anguish, this time as the events of the past night came back to her, one by one, in all their horrifying details. Her labor of love, begun the night before, was not yet ended. The parcel containing the watch and money were there beneath her, pressing into her bosom. When she managed to regain her feet the first thing which she did was to rekindle the fire with splinters of pine and pieces of hickory that were at hand in her wood box. When the fire was burning briskly, Tante Elodie took the paper money from the little bundle and burned it. She did not notice the denomination of the bills, there were five or six, she thrust them into the blaze with the poker and watched them burn. The few loose pieces of silver she put in her purse, apart from her own money; there was sixty-five cents in small coin. The watch she placed between her mattresses; then, seized with misgiving, took it out. She gazed around the room, seeking a safe hiding place and finally put the watch into a large, strong stocking which she pinned securely around her waist beneath her clothing. The knife she washed carefully, drying it with pieces of newspaper which she burned. The water in which she had washed it she also threw in a corner of the large fire place upon a heap of ashes. Then she put the knife into the pocket of one of Gabriel's coats which she had cleaned and mended for him; it was hanging in her closet.

She did all this slowly and with great effort, for she felt very sick. When the unpleasant work was over it was all she could do to undress and get beneath the covers of her bed.

She knew that when she did not appear at breakfast Madame Nicolas would send to investigate the cause of her absence. She took her meals with the young widow around the corner of the gallery. Tante Elodie was not rich. She received a small income from the remains of what had once been a magnificent plantation adjoining the lands which Justin Lucaze owned and cultivated. But she lived frugally, with a hundred small cares and economies and rarely felt the want of extra money except when the generosity of her nature prompted her to help an afflicted neighbor, or to bestow a gift upon some one of whom she was fond. It often seemed to Tante Elodie that all the affection of her heart was centered upon her young protégé, Gabriel; that what she felt for others was simply an emanation—rays, as it were, from this central sun of love that shone for him alone.

In the midst of twinges, of nervous tremors, her thoughts were with him. It was impossible for her to think of anything else. She was filled with unspeakable dread that he might betray himself. She wondered what he had done after he left her: what he was doing at that moment? She wanted to see him again alone, to insist anew upon the necessity of his self-assertion of innocence.

As she expected, Mrs. Wm. Nicolas came around at the breakfast hour to see what was the matter. She was an active woman, very pretty and fresh looking, with willing, deft hands and the kindest voice and eyes. She was distressed at the spectacle of poor Tante Elodie extended in bed with her head tied up, and looking pale and suffering.

"Ah! I suspected it!" she exclaimed, "coming out in the cold on the gallery last night to get morphine for Gabriel; *ma foi!* as if he could not go to the drug store for his morphine! Where have you pain? Have you any fever, Tante Elodie?"

"It is nothing, *chérie*. I believe I am only tired and want to rest for a day in bed."

"Then you must rest as long as you want. I will look after your fire and see that you have what you need. I will bring your coffee at once. It is a beautiful day; like spring. When the sun gets very warm I will open the window."

## V

All day long Gabriel did not appear, and she dared not make inquiries about him. Several persons came in to see her, learning that she was sick. The midnight murder in the Nigger-Luke Cabin seemed to be the favorite subject of conversation among her visitors. They were not greatly excited over it as they might have been were the man other than a comparative stranger. But the subject seemed full of interest, enhanced by the mystery surrounding it. Madame Nicolas did not risk to speak of it.

"That is not a fit conversation for a sick-room. Any doctor—anybody with sense will tell you. For Mercy's sake! change the subject."

But Fifine Delonce could not be silenced.

"And now it appears," she went on with renewed animation, "it appears he was playing cards down at Symund's store. That shows how they pass their time—those boys! It's a scandal! But nobody can remember when he left. Some say at nine, some say it was past eleven. He sort of went away like he didn't want them to notice."

"Well, we didn't know the man. My patience! there are murders every day. If we had to keep up with them, *ma foi!* Who is going to Lucie's card party tomorrow? I hear she did not invite her cousin Claire. They have fallen out again it seems." And Madame Nicolas, after speaking, went to give Tante Elodie a drink of *Tisane*.

"Mr. Ben's got about twenty darkies from Niggerville, holding them on suspicion," continued Fifine, dancing on the edge of her chair. "Without doubt the man was enticed to the cabin and murdered and robbed there. Not a picayune left in his pockets! only his pistol—that they didn't take, all loaded, in his back pocket, that he might have used, and his watch gone!

Mr. Ben thinks his brother in Conshotta, that's very well off, is going to offer a big reward."

"What relation was the man to you, Fifine?" asked Madame Nicolas, sarcastically.

"He was a human being, Amelia; you have no heart, no feeling. If it makes a woman that hard to associate with a doctor, then thank God—well—as I was saying, if they can catch those two strange section hands that left town last night—but you better bet they're not such fools to keep that watch. But old Uncle Marte said he saw little foot prints like a woman's early this morning, but no one wanted to listen to him or pay any attention, and the crowd tramped them out in little or no time. None of the boys want to let on; they don't want us to know which ones were playing cards at Symund's. Was Gabriel at Symund's, Tante Elodie?"

Tante Elodie coughed painfully and looked blankly as though she had only heard her name and had been inattentive to what was said.

"For pity sake leave Tante Elodie out of this! it's bad enough she has to listen, suffering as she is. Gabriel spent the evening here, on Tante Elodie's sofa, very sick with cramps. You will have to pursue your detective work in some other quarter, my dear."

A little girl came in with a huge bunch of blossoms. There was some bustle attending the arrangement of the flowers in vases, and in the midst of it, two or three ladies took their leave.

"I wonder if they're going to send the body off to-night, or if they're going to keep it for the morning train," Fifine was heard to speculate, before the door closed upon her.

Tante Elodie could not sleep that night. The following day she had some fever and Madame Nicolas insisted upon her seeing the doctor. He gave her a sleeping draught and some fever drops and said she would be all right in a few days; for he could find nothing alarming in her condition.

By a supreme effort of the will she got up on the third day hoping in the accustomed routine of her daily life to get rid, in part, of the uneasiness and unhappiness that possessed her.

The sun shone warm in the afternoon and she went and stood on the gallery watching for Gabriel to pass. He had not been near her. She was wounded, alarmed, miserable at his silence and absence; but determined to see him. He came down the street, presently, never looking up, with his hat drawn over his eyes.

"Gabriel!" she called. He gave a start and glanced around.

"Come up; I want to see you a moment."

"I haven't time now, Tante Elodie."

"Come in!" she said sharply.

"All right, you'll have to fix it up with Morrison," and he opened the gate and went in. She was back in her room by the time he reached it, and in her chair, trembling a little and feeling sick again.

"Gabriel, if you 'ave no heart, it seems to me you would 'ave some intelligence; a moment's reflection would show you the folly of altering your 'abits so suddenly. Did you not know I was sick? did you not guess my uneasiness?"

"I haven't guessed anything or known anything but a taste of hell," he said, not looking at her. Her heart bled afresh for him and went out to him in full forgiveness. "You were right," he went on, "it would have been horrible to say anything. There is no suspicion. I'll never say anything unless some one should be falsely accused."

"There will be no possible evidence to accuse anyone," she assured him. "Forget it, forget it. Keep on as though it was something you had dreamed. Not only for the outside, but within yourself. Do not accuse yourself of that act, but the actions, the conduct, the ungovernable temper that made it possible. Promise me it will be a lesson to you, Gabriel; and God, who reads men's hearts, will not call it a crime, but an accident which your unbridled nature invited. I will forget it. You must forget it. 'Ave you been to the office?"

"Today; not yesterday. I don't know what I did yesterday, but look for the knife—after they—I couldn't go while he was there—and I thought every minute some one was coming to accuse me. And when I realized they weren't—I don't know—I drank too much, I think. Reading law! I might as well have been reading Hebrew. If Morrison thinks—See here Tante Elodie, are there any spots on this coat? Can you see anything here in the light?"

"There are no spots anywhere. Stop thinking of it, I implore you." But he pulled off the coat and flung it across a chair. He went to the closet to get his other coat which he knew hung there. Tante Elodie, still feeble and suffering, in the depths of her chair, was not quick enough, could think of no way to prevent it. She had at first put the knife in his pocket with the intention of returning it to him. But now she dreaded to have him find it, and thus discover the part she had played in the sickening dream.

He buttoned up his coat briskly and started away.

"Please burn it," he said, looking at the garment on the chair, "I never want to see it again."

## VI

When it became distinctly evident that no slightest suspicion would be attached to him for the killing of Everson; when he plainly realized that there was no one upon whom the guilt could be fastened, Gabriel thought he would regain his lost equilibrium. If in no other way, he fancied he could reason himself back into it. He was suffering, but he someway had no fear that his present condition of mind would last. He thought it would pass away like a malignant fever. It would have to pass away or it would have to kill him.

From Tante Elodie's he went over to Morrison's office where he was reading law. Morrison and his partner were out of town and he had the office to himself. He had been there all morning. There was nothing for him to do now but to see anyone who called on business, and to go on with his reading. He seated himself and spread his book before him, but he looked into the street through the open door. Then he got up and shut the door. He again fastened his eyes upon the pages before him, but his mind was traveling other ways. For the hundredth time he was going over every detail of the fatal night, and trying to justify himself in his own heart.

If it had been an open and fair fight there would have been no trouble in squaring himself with his conscience; if the man had shown the slightest disposition to do him bodily harm, but he had not. On the other hand, he asked himself, what constituted a murder? Why, there was Morrison himself who had once fired at Judge Filips on that very street. His ball had gone wide of the mark, and subsequently he and Filips had adjusted their difficulties and become friends. Was Morrison any less a murderer because his weapon had missed?

Suppose the knife had swerved, had penetrated the arm, had inflicted a harmless scratch or flesh wound, would he be sitting there now, calling himself names? But he would try to think it all out later. He could not bear to be there alone, he never liked to be alone, and now he could not endure it. He closed the book without the slightest recollection of a line his eyes had followed. He went and gazed up and down the street, then he locked the office and walked away.

The fact of Everson having been robbed was very puzzling to Gabriel. He thought about it as he walked along the street.

The complete change that had taken place in his emotions, his sentiments, did not astonish him in the least: we accept such phenomena without question. A week ago—not so long as that—he was in love with the fair-haired girl up at the Normal. He was undeniably in love with her. He knew the symptoms. He wanted to marry her and meant to ask her whenever his position justified him in doing so.

Now, where had that love gone? He thought of her with indifference. Still, he was seeking her at that moment, through habit, without any special motive. He had no positive desire to see her; to see any one; and yet he could not endure to be alone. He had no desire to see Tante Elodie. She wanted him to forget and her presence made him remember.

The girl was walking under the beautiful trees, and she stood and waited for him, when she saw him mounting the hill. As he looked at her, his fondness for her and his intentions toward her, appeared now, like child's play. Life was something terrible of which she had no conception. She seemed to him as harmless, as innocent, as insignificant as a little bird.

"Oh! Gabriel," she exclaimed. "I had just written you a note. Why haven't you been here? It was foolish to get offended. I wanted to explain: I couldn't get out of it the other night, at Tante Elodie's, when he asked me. You know I couldn't, and that I would rather have come with you." Was it possible he would have taken this seriously a week ago?

"Delonce is a good fellow; he's a decent fellow. I don't blame you. That's all right." She was hurt at his easy complaisance. She did not wish to offend him, and here she was grieved because he was not offended.

"Will you come indoors to the fire?" she asked.

"No; I just strolled up for a minute." He leaned against a

tree and looked bored, or rather, preoccupied with other things than herself. It was not a week ago that he wanted to see her every day; when he said the hours were like minutes that he passed beside her. "I just strolled up to tell you that I am going away."

"Oh! going away?" and the pink deepened in her cheeks, and she tried to look indifferent and to clasp her glove tighter. He had not the slightest intention of going away when he mounted the hill. It came to him like an inspiration.

"Where are you going?"

"Going to look for work in the city."

"And what about your law studies?"

"I have no talent for the law; it's about time I acknowledged it. I want to get into something that will make me hustle. I wouldn't mind—I'd like to get something to do on a railroad that would go tearing through the country night and day. What's the matter?" he asked, perceiving the tears that she could not conceal.

"Nothing's the matter," she answered with dignity, and a sense of seeming proud.

He took her word for it and, instead of seeking to console her, went rambling on about the various occupations in which he should like to engage for a while.

"When are you going?"

"Just as soon as I can."

"Shall I see you again?"

"Of course. Good-bye. Don't stay out here too long; you might take cold." He listlessly shook hands with her and descended the hill with long rapid strides.

He would not intentionally have hurt her. He did not realize that he was wounding her. It would have been as difficult for him to revive his passion for her as to bring Everson back to life. Gabriel knew there could be fresh horror added to the situation. Discovery would have added to it; a false accusation would have deepened it. But he never dreamed of the new horror coming as it did, through Tante Elodie, when he found the knife in his pocket. It took a long time to realize what it meant; and then he felt as if he never wanted to see her again. In his mind, her action identified itself with his crime, and made itself a hateful, hideous part of it, which he could not endure to think of, and of which he could not help thinking.

It was the one thing which had saved him, and yet he felt no gratitude. The great love which had prompted the deed did not soften him. He could not believe that any man was worth loving to such length, or worth saving at such a price. She seemed, to his imagination, less a woman than a monster, capable of committing, in cold-blood, deeds, which he himself could only accomplish in blind rage. For the first time, Gabriel wept. He threw himself down upon the ground in the deepening twilight and wept as he never had before in his life. A terrible sense of loss overpowered him; as if someone dearer than a mother had been taken out of the reach of his heart; as if a refuge had gone from him. The last spark of human affection was dead within him. He knew it as he was losing it. He wept at the loss which left him alone with his thoughts.

## VII

Tante Elodie was always chilly. It was warm for the last of April, and the women at Madame Nicolas's wedding were all in airy summer attire. All but Tante Elodie, who wore her black silk, her old silk with a white lace fichu, and she held an embroidered handkerchief and a fan in her hand.

Fifine Delonce had been over in the morning to take up the seams in the dress, for, as she expressed herself, it was miles too loose for Tante Elodie's figure. She appeared to be shrivelling away to nothing. She had not again been sick in bed since that little spell in February; but she was plainly wasting and was very feeble. Her eyes, though, were as bright as ever; sometimes they looked as hard as flint. The doctor, whom Madame Nicolas insisted upon her seeing occasionally, gave a name to her disease; it was a Greek name and sounded convincing. She was taking a tonic especially prepared for her, from a large bottle, three times a day.

Fifine was a great gossip. When and how she gathered her news nobody could tell. It was always said she knew ten times more than the weekly paper would dare to print. She often visited Tante Elodie, and she told her news of everyone; among others of Gabriel.

It was she who told that he had abandoned the study of the law. She told Tante Elodie when he started for the city to look for work and when he came back from the fruitless search.

"Did you know that Gabriel is working on the railroad, now? Fireman! Think of it! What a comedown from reading law in Morrison's office. If I were a man, I'd try to have more strength of character than to go to the dogs on account of a girl; an insignificant somebody from Kansas! Even if she is going to marry my brother, I must say it was no way to treat a boy—leading him on, especially a boy like Gabriel, that any girl would have been glad—Well, it's none of my business; only I'm sorry he took it like he did. Drinking himself to death, they say."

That morning, as she was taking up the seams of the silk dress, there was fresh news of Gabriel. He was tired of the railroad, it seemed. He was down on his father's place herding cattle, breaking in colts, drinking like a fish.

"I wouldn't have such a thing on my conscience! Goodness me! I couldn't sleep at nights if I was that girl."

Tante Elodie always listened with a sad, resigned smile. It did not seem to make any difference whether she had Gabriel or not. He had broken her heart and he was killing her. It was not his crime that had broken her heart; it was his indifference to her love and his turning away from her.

It was whispered about that Tante Elodie had grown indifferent to her religion. There was no truth in it. She had not been to confession for two months; but otherwise she followed closely the demands made upon her; redoubling her zeal in church work and attending mass each morning.

At the wedding she was holding quite a little reception of her own in the corner of the gallery. The air was mild and pleasant. Young people flocked about her and occasionally the radiant bride came out to see if she were comfortable and if there was anything she wanted to eat or drink.

A young girl leaning over the railing suddenly exclaimed "*Tiens!* someone is dead. I didn't know any one was sick." She was watching the approach of a man who was coming down the street, distributing, according to the custom of the country, a death notice from door to door.

He wore a long black coat and walked with a measured tread. He was as expressionless as an automaton; handing the little slips of paper at every door; not missing one. The girl, leaning over the railing, went to the head of the stairs to receive the notice when he entered Tante Elodie's gate.

The small, single sheet, which he gave her, was bordered in black and decorated with an old-fashioned wood cut of a weeping willow beside a grave. It was an announcement on the part of Monsieur Justin Lucaze of the death of his only son, Gabriel, who had been instantly killed, the night before, by a fall from his horse.

If the automaton had had any sense of decency, he might have skipped the house of joy, in which there was a wedding feast, in which there was the sound of laughter, the click of glasses, the hum of merry voices, and a vision of sweet women with their thoughts upon love and marriage and earthly bliss. But he had no sense of decency. He was as indifferent and relentless as Death, whose messenger he was.

The sad news, passed from lip to lip, cast a shadow as if a cloud had flitted across the sky. Tante Elodie alone stayed in its shadow. She sank deeper down into the rocker, more shrivelled than ever. They all remembered Tante Elodie's romance and respected her grief.

She did not speak any more, or even smile, but wiped her forehead with the old lace handkerchief and sometimes closed her eyes. When she closed her eyes she pictured Gabriel dead, down there on the plantation, with his father watching beside him. He might have betrayed himself had he lived. There was nothing now to betray him. Even the shining gold watch lay deep in a gorged ravine where she had flung it when she once walked through the country alone at dusk.

She thought of her own place down there beside Justin's, all dismantled, with bats beating about the eaves and negroes living under the falling roof.

Tante Elodie did not seem to want to go in doors again. The bride and groom went away. The guests went away, one by one, and all the little children. She stayed there alone in the corner, under the deep shadow of the oaks while the stars came out to keep her company.

"The Godmother." Written January–February 6, 1899. Published in *St. Louis Mirror* (December 12, 1901).

# NOTES

### *A Vocation and a Voice*

1.8–9 *Woodland Park.* Kate Chopin is alluding to Forest Park, St. Louis's first public park, opened in 1876 on a heavily wooded 1375-acre tract just west of Kingshighway. The St. Louis World's Fair (Louisiana Purchase Exposition) of 1904 was held in Forest Park, and it was during the Fair that Kate Chopin had the cerebral hemorrhage that killed her.

2.18 *"The Patch."* Kerry Patch, the Irish ghetto in St. Louis. Chopin's father, the Irish immigrant Thomas O'Flaherty, was a contributor to charities for "The Patch," and Kate O'Flaherty (later Chopin) spent one school year as a special music student at the Academy of the Visitation, a convent school known as "The

Castle of Kerry Patch." Her friend William Marion Reedy (see Introduction, this volume) grew up in Kerry Patch.

5.17 *movers*. Itinerants or vagabonds. The 1893 financial panic, one of the most devastating economic depressions in American history, made many people homeless.

7.13 *nicks-com-araus*. Gibberish or meaningless talk, from the German *nichts kommt heraus*. I am grateful to Irene di Maio for this translation.

7.14 *Dutch*. Deutsch, i.e., Germans. St. Louisans often called the German-American immigrants "Dutch": in an 1864 letter, Kate O'Flaherty's mother complained about a "compy of dutch devils" who celebrated the Union victory at Vicksburg by invading her home and forcing her, at bayonet point, to hoist a flag.

8.12 *measly truck*. Shabby possessions of little value.

9.10–11 *He might have been Egyptian, for aught the boy could guess, or Zulu*. "Egyptian" was a general term for anyone or anything exotic that seemed to come from the Middle East. "Zulu" was a general term for anyone or anything seeming to be African. Gypsies were sometimes written up in St. Louis newspapers, but Chopin deliberately makes Gutro's ethnic background obscure.

9.14 *oriental*. Used for anything exotic that might have come from the Middle East.

9.32 *menage*. A household or family arrangement.

15.27 *lagniappe*. (*lan-yap*). A little something extra, a bonus.

16.13 *bayou*. A stream, sometimes sluggish or marshy. Chopin's use of this term and her mention of crawfish identify the setting as Louisiana.

16.15 *crawfishes*. Small, spiny creatures resembling tiny lobsters. They live in ditches and bayous and are one of the staples of Acadian (Cajun) food in Louisiana. In other parts of the country, they are sometimes called crayfish, crawdads, or mudbugs.

17.17–18 *Judica me, Deus, et discerna causam meam, de gente non sancta—ab homine iniquo et doloso erue me*. "Vindicate me, O Lord, and defend my cause against an ungodly people—from deceitful and unjust men deliver me" (Psalms 43:1). These lines are a part of the prayers recited by the priest at the foot of the altar in the old Latin Mass. Until the mid-1960s, Roman Catholic masses around the world were said in Latin. I am grateful to John R. May for aiding me with this passage.

17.30 *'Cadian*. "Cajun," a descendant of French-Canadian settlers in Acadia, Nova Scotia, who were expelled from Canada in 1755 because they refused to swear allegiance to the English government. After much wandering, as described in Henry Wadsworth Longfellow's poem "Evangeline," they settled in south Louisiana.

18.1 *mixed congregation of whites and blacks*. In the 1890s most southern Protestant churches and denominations were for blacks only, or whites only. But Catholic churches, like Kate Chopin's St. John the Baptist Church in Cloutierville, Louisiana, were integrated. Sometimes there were separate doors for blacks and whites to enter, and even a third door for "people of color" or "mulattoes" (those of mixed race).

21.29 *canonicals*. Clothing worn while serving mass.

22.31–32 *the priest in his slow, careful, broken English*. Here Chopin may be recalling Father Jean Marie Beaulieu, the village priest she knew in Cloutierville, who was

French-born and more at home in French than in English.

24.6 *nostrums*. Patent or quack medicines.

24.12 *specifics*. Medicines intended for particular diseases or conditions.

24.28–29 *catch-penny*. Quick, cheap ways of making money.

27.9 *ablutions*. Washings of the body.

34.7 *the "Refuge."* The monastery.

34.21 *You'll not be telling me*. This pattern of speech indicates that the speaker is Irish-American—as does "It's a prison he'll be putting us in," two paragraphs later. In St. Louis, as in other cities, Irishmen were apt to become priests, policemen, or politicians.

## Elizabeth Stock's One Story

37.2 *consumption*. Tuberculosis.

40.16–17 *To a person that knew B. from hill's foot*. Rustic expression meaning "anyone who knew anything at all."

## Two Portraits

48.27 *intercourse with the all-wise and all-seeing God*. "Intercourse" in nineteenth-century writings means "conversation" or "interaction."

49.29 *numbers*. Numbers of people.

## A Mental Suggestion

57.4 *Tennis-Girl*. A young woman who played tennis. Athletics for women were a new and popular pursuit in the 1890s, and women were sometimes identified by the sports they preferred.

57.8 *Glasgow men . . . Persian tapestry that seems like a Hornel*. The kinds of artists and artwork that Pauline collected. Oriental rugs and hangings were popular among wealthy people in the late nineteenth-century in the United States.

57.13 *Golf-Girl*. See "Tennis-Girl," above.

59.13–14 *Lilienthal about the Tintoretto*. Lilienthal is evidently an art dealer; Tintoretto (1518–94) was a Venetian painter.

63.13–14 *palsied his resolution*. Prevented him from taking action.

63.32 *pince-nez*. Eyeglasses without earpieces, kept in place by a spring that grips the bridge of the nose. Kate Chopin wore them in a 1900 newspaper sketch by her son Oscar, and so did her friend Florence Hayward in many newspaper caricatures.

64.7 *ménage*. A household or family arrangement.

64.9 *some patriarch of old*. Graham's grandiose fantasies link him with Abraham of the Old Testament, asked by God to prove his faith by sacrificing his son Isaac.

## An Egyptian Cigarette

67.7 *fakir*. A Moslem or Hindu itinerant beggar, often reputedly able to perform miracles.

68.5–6 *Turkish or ordinary Egyptian*. Turkish and Egyptian were two of the most popular kinds of tobacco at the turn of the century. In its name and pictures, Camel cigarettes drew on this fascination with "Orientalism."

68.10 *smoking-den*. Wealthy people often confined smoking to one room of a large house. Few women smoked; Kate Chopin, who enjoyed Cuban cigarettes, was an exception—and on one occasion, she reportedly received guests while in the bathtub, smoking a big black cigar. Men generally preferred cigars to cigarettes: in *The Awakening* (chapter II), Robert explains that he is smoking cigarettes because he cannot afford cigars. The unhealthy effects of smoking were already being reported in late nineteenth-century newspapers.

68.13 *oriental*. The sultry image of the Orient—hot, indolent, decadent, full of wisdom and sensuality—appealed to many artists and writers at the turn of the century. "Orient" generally meant the Middle East.

68.18 *complete paraphernalia of a smoker*. These would include rolling papers, matches, tobacco, and pipes, possibly including hookahs (water pipes). Kate Chopin's friend William Vincent Byars was a collector of oddly shaped pipes.

68.25 *the Egyptian cigarette*. Presumably hashish, possibly laced with opium (according to the 1960s-era experts I consulted). Taking an "inspiration" means inhaling.

69.18 *Bardja*. Evidently an Oriental god, probably invented by Chopin. I am grateful to Marilyn Bonnell for trying to find other sources using the name Bardja.

## The Night Came Slowly

85.9 *necromancer's spell*. A sorcerer or magician's work.

## Juanita

86.3 *Rock Springs*. Evidently a small town in rural Missouri.

86.10 *"Mother Hubbard."* A full loose gown for women, similar to a muumuu.

88.1 *soliciting subscriptions*. Collecting money.

## The Unexpected

92.19 *mounted her "wheel."* Bicycles were known as "wheels." Bicycling, extremely popular among young women of the 1890s, was a sign of the New Woman's emancipation from old domestic ways. O. K. Bovard, a visitor to Kate Chopin's salon, wrote a bicycling column for a St. Louis newspaper.

## Her Letters

100.13–14 *the bridge that spanned the river—the deep, broad, swift, black river dividing two States*. Possibly the Eads Bridge, which spans the Mississippi River at St. Louis, between Missouri and Illinois. Kate Chopin attended the grand opening of the Eads Bridge in 1874.

## The Kiss

105.9 *brune type*. Brunette type.

## Suzette

109.3 *Ah, bon Dieu!* "Oh, dear God!"
109.3–4 *c' pauv' Michel!* "That poor Michel!"
109.5–6 *Chartrand's "hands."* Field workers. Chartrand is the name of a shopkeeper in Chopin's first novel, *At Fault*; she named him for Charles Bertrand, a Cloutierville store owner she knew.
109.6 *the cut-off*. A road or passage that shortens a distance; a shortcut.
109.8 *fagots*. Bundles of twigs, sticks, or branches.
109.13 *Grand Ecore flat*. The flatboat from Grand Ecore, Louisiana, a Cane River (Natchitoches Parish) country settlement where some of Kate Chopin's relatives lived. Louisiana has parishes instead of counties.
110.11 *Red River*. A river in northwest Louisiana, flowing through northern Natchitoches Parish.
110.18 *Michel Jardeau est mort!* "Michel Jardeau is dead!"
110.24–25 *finish her toilet*. Finish her dressing and grooming.
112.26–27 *Mère de Dieu!* "Mother of God!"

## The Recovery

119.29 *bonhomme*. "Gentleman."

## Lilacs

131.13 *cabriolet*. A light, two-wheeled carriage.
132.20 *Sacré-Coeur*. The Sacred Heart, a holy image among Catholics. This picture indicates that the story is taking place in a convent run by nuns of the Society of

the Sacred Heart. Kate O'Flaherty (later Chopin) attended the Sacred Heart Academy in St. Louis with her friend Kitty Garesché, who became a Sacred Heart nun. Chopin also mentions visiting another school friend, a Sacred Heart nun, in her 1894 diary (reprinted in *Kate Chopin's Private Papers*).

132.21 *Ste. Catherine de Sienne*. St. Catherine of Siena, an Italian nun and famous mystic (1347–1380). Kate O'Flaherty (Chopin) may have been named after her.

133.30 *refectory*. Dining hall in an institution.

134.7 *lay sisters*. Women who did domestic duties for the Sacred Heart nuns. Often they came from a lower class background than the women who became Sacred Heart nuns.

135.14 *ma tante de Sierge*. "My aunt from Sierge," evidently one of Sister Agathe's memories of home.

135.30 *enragée*. A mad woman.

136.17 *St. Lazare*. A mental asylum.

137.14 *angelus bell*. The bell announcing the Angelus, a prayer said at morning, noon, and evening and beginning with the words "Angelus Domini."

137.26–27 *Jacob's dream at the foot of the ladder*. Refers to Jacob's dream of a ladder from earth to heaven in Genesis 28.

137.30 *bénitiers*. Holy water basins.

138.26 *fortnight*. Two weeks.

139.2–3 *it was as far as she might go*. Nuns were cloistered, not permitted to leave their convents and grounds, until Vatican II (the Roman Catholic ecumenical councils held in 1962–1965). For the Sacred Heart nuns, buying groceries and other chores involving trips to the world outside the convent were handled by lay sisters.

139.10 *negligé*. Negligee, a woman's loosely fitting, flowing gown; often the word connotes informal or careless dress.

139.23 *ennui*. Boredom.

140.1 *La Petite Gilberta*. "The Little Gilberta": Adrienne's rival in the Paris opera.

140.2 *like a traînée of a café chantant*. "Like a trainee in a musical café," presumably with singing performers: Sophie is claiming that La Petite Gilberta has no talent.

140.9 *dainties*. Choice foods, delicacies.

140.12 *watering-place*. A resort with a spa or springs. Kate Chopin's husband, Oscar, tried to recover his health at Hot Springs, Arkansas, in the year before his death.

140.28 *Mons. Zola!* Emile Zola (1840–1902), French writer of long, detailed novels critical of the ruling class and religious hypocrisies. Kate Chopin considered his writings heavy and dull, overly researched and too obviously intended to instruct and preach. She said that his *Lourdes* was "swamped beneath a mass of prosaic data, offensive and nauseous description and rampant sentimentality." Since Zola was considered something of an enemy of the Catholic Church and *Lourdes* was reportedly banned, the presence of his book in Adrienne's room suggests that she (or Sophie) is not a devout believer. Chopin wrote "Lilacs" on May 14–16, 1894; her review of Emile Zola's *Lourdes* appeared in *St. Louis Life* on November 17, 1894; and between November 18–22 she wrote the story "A Sentimental Soul," which includes an irascible opinionated character named Lacodie, who is much like Emile Zola.

141.11 *désolé*. Desolated; emotionally distressed.

141.16 *chiffonier*. A chest of drawers or narrow, high bureau.

141.24 *Ma foi!* "Really!" "To be sure!"

141.33 *Château Yquem*. Château d'Yquem, a French white wine from Bordeaux.

142.1 *cigarettes*. Her smoking defines Adrienne as a woman of the world, with decadent tastes.

142.8 *bonne*. Maid or domestic servant.

142.24 *majolica pitcher*. Majolica is a type of Italian pottery that is enameled, glazed, and decorated with rich colors.

142.28 *peignoir*. A woman's full, loose, dressing gown, similar to a negligee.

## *Ti Démon (A Horse Story)*

147.3 *'Cadian*. Cajun. See above.

147.3 *Bayou Derbanne*. Now called Bayou D'Arbonne, this bayou is south of Natchitoches, Louisiana.

147.10 *garden truck*. Garden vegetables.

147.12 *Ti Démon*. "Little Devil." In Acadian (Cajun) French, *ti* is short for *petit*, meaning "little."

148.3 *Allons donc!* "Come now!" "Nonsense!"

148.17 *Courage!* "Cheer up!" "Take courage!"

149.1 *observing the toilets*. Learning the grooming and dressing habits.

149.15 *grosse bête!* "You big beast, you!"

156.10 *the Sabine*. The Sabine River separates part of western Louisiana from east Texas.

156.23 *couche-couche*. Ground corn.

## *Ti Démon*

157.6 *'Cadian Bayou*. A bayou (probably fictitious) near Ti Démon's home.

157.7 *endimanché*. Wearing their best clothes, dressed in their Sunday best (*dimanche* is French for Sunday).

157.12 *cornet*. A horn-shaped container or cone.

158.3 *Plaisance*. The name means "pleasure."

158.3–4 *Ti Démon*. Little Devil.

158.11 *rendez-vouz*. Rendezvous, or meeting.

158.18–19 *savon fin*. Fine soap.

159.12–13 *seven-up*. A card game for two, three, or four people in which seven points constitute a game.

160.5 *gallery*. A long porch that encircles a house.

160.6 *brogans*. Heavy work shoes that fit high on the ankle.

161.27 *Au Secours!* "Help!"

162.19 *blunderbuss*. A cumbersome, short gun with a broad, flaring muzzle, accurate only at very close range.

162.31–32 *il est bien nommé Ti Démon, va!* "He's well-named Little Devil, yes!"

163.2 *mine out!* Watch out!

## *The Godmother*

164.5 *gallery*. A long porch encircling a house.

164.13 *Normal school*. The teachers' college in Natchitoches, Louisiana, now Northwestern State University of Louisiana. The town is pronounced *Nack-i-tush*. As indicated later in the story, the "Normal" had an excellent reputation for teacher training, and it attracted many students from out of state.

165.5 *cribbage*. A card game. Kate Chopin loved card playing, especially euchre (a form of bridge), and called herself a "euchre fiend." Her daughter Lélia made a career as a teacher and writer about bridge, backgammon, and other games.

165.7 *pralines*. Crisp candies made of nuts, brown sugar, and sweet syrup.

165.16 *rubber*. A series of games.

165.22 *muffler*. Neck scarf.

167.8 "*solitaire*." Any card game played by one person. Kate Chopin's fondness for solitaire was noted in the St. Louis newspapers.

167.16 *ambrotype*. A photograph made by an old process, in which a glass negative was backed with a dark surface, so that it appeared positive.

168.11 *peignoir*. A loose, flowing gown, sometimes a robe.

168.16–17 *her Notre Père, her Salve Marie, and Je crois en Dieu*. Three prayers said in the rosary: "Our Father," "Hail Mary," and the Apostles' Creed, which begins "I believe in God."

168.20 *Vierge des Vierges: Priez pour nous. Mère de Dieu: Priez—* "Virgin of Virgins: Pray for us. Mother of God: Pray—" Tante Elodie is saying her rosary.

168.24 *old town*. Natchitoches, founded in 1714, is the oldest town in Louisiana.

168.32 *Qui est là?* "Who's there?"

169.29 *Boute!* An exclamation of doubt.

170.22 *Conshotta*. Chopin probably meant Coushatta, a town north of Natchitoches.

173.1 *chérie*. "Dear one" or "honey."

173.3 *morphine*. In the nineteenth century morphine, which was virtually unregulated, was used at home for many ailments, including stomach pains, rheumatism, and menstrual cramps.

177.21–22 *ma foi!* "Now, really!"

178.26 *Tisane.* An herbal tea, often for medicinal purposes.

178.27 *twenty darkies from Niggerville.* White people frequently used this kind of language to refer to blacks or African-Americans.

178.30 *picayune.* A French coin of small value.

179.33 *sleeping draught.* A medicine to enable her to sleep.

181.10 *Reading law.* Gabriel has apprenticed himself to Morrison, a lawyer who will guide his reading and teach him what he needs to know to become an attorney. "Reading law" was once much more common than attending law school. Kate Chopin's brother-in-law Phanor Breazeale read law and was later elected to political office.

185.27 *white lace fichu.* A three-cornered cape for women, with the ends fastened or crossed in front.

187.17 *Tiens!* "Look here!"

## FOR THE BEST IN PAPERBACKS, LOOK FOR THE 

In every corner of the world, on every subject under the sun, Penguin represents quality and variety—the very best in publishing today.

For complete information about books available from Penguin—including Puffins, Penguin Classics, and Arkana—and how to order them, write to us at the appropriate address below. Please note that for copyright reasons the selection of books varies from country to country.

---

**In the United Kingdom:** Please write to *Dept. JC, Penguin Books Ltd, FREEPOST, West Drayton, Middlesex UB7 0BR*.

If you have any difficulty in obtaining a title, please send your order with the correct money, plus ten percent for postage and packaging, to *P.O. Box No. 11, West Drayton, Middlesex UB7 0BR*

**In the United States:** Please write to *Consumer Sales, Penguin USA, P.O. Box 999, Dept. 17109, Bergenfield, New Jersey 07621-0120*. VISA and MasterCard holders call 1-800-253-6476 to order all Penguin titles

**In Canada:** Please write to *Penguin Books Canada Ltd, 10 Alcorn Avenue, Suite 300, Toronto, Ontario M4V 3B2*

**In Australia:** Please write to *Penguin Books Australia Ltd, P.O. Box 257, Ringwood, Victoria 3134*

**In New Zealand:** Please write to *Penguin Books (NZ) Ltd, Private Bag 102902, North Shore Mail Centre, Auckland 10*

**In India:** Please write to *Penguin Books India Pvt Ltd, 706 Eros Apartments, 56 Nehru Place, New Delhi 110 019*

**In the Netherlands:** Please write to *Penguin Books Netherlands bv, Postbus 3507, NL-1001 AH Amsterdam*

**In Germany:** Please write to *Penguin Books Deutschland GmbH, Metzlerstrasse 26, 60594 Frankfurt am Main*

**In Spain:** Please write to *Penguin Books S.A., Bravo Murillo 19, 1° B, 28015 Madrid*

**In Italy:** Please write to *Penguin Italia s.r.l., Via Felice Casati 20, I-20124 Milano*

**In France:** Please write to *Penguin France S. A., 17 rue Lejeune, F-31000 Toulouse*

**In Japan:** Please write to *Penguin Books Japan, Ishikiribashi Building, 2–5–4, Suido, Bunkyo-ku, Tokyo 112*

**In Greece:** Please write to *Penguin Hellas Ltd, Dimocritou 3, GR–106 71 Athens*

**In South Africa:** Please write to *Longman Penguin Southern Africa (Pty) Ltd, Private Bag X08, Bertsham 2013*

Chopin, Kate, 1851-
1904.

A vocation and a
voice.

| DATE | | | |
|---|---|---|---|
| 10/28/03 | 3/23/06 | | |
| 3/16/04 | | | |
| 10/20/04 | | | |
| 6/9/05 | | | |
| 10/30/05 | | | |
| 3/1/06 | | | |